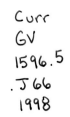

DANCE

WRITTEN BY
BILL T. JONES
AND SUSAN KUKLIN

PHOTOGRAPHED BY
SUSAN KUKLIN

HYPERION BOOKS FOR CHILDREN
New York

I am a dancer.
I want to dance.

When I dance,

I use parts of me,

and I use all of me.

Before I dance,

*I warm
my body,*

and I stretch my body.

I want to dance.

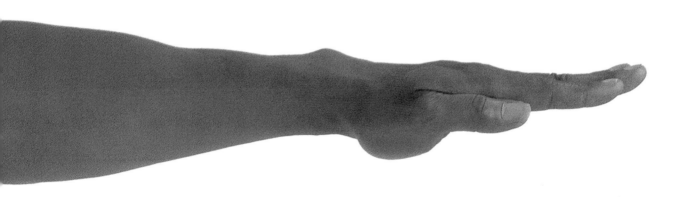

When I am dancing,
I can make lines,

and I can make curves.

When I am dancing,
I can fly high

and soar through the air.

But I've got to come down

and dance on the ground.

When I am dancing,
I am thinking

and I am feeling.

When I am dancing

I am everywhere,

and I am hardly there.

INTRODUCTION

Photography is not about focal lengths, film speeds and f-stops, it is about images. What you point your camera at, what you include within its viewfinder, what negative you make into a print, and what context you place that print in. This book attempts to explain and illustrate what photographs are and how they are used today.

The Eastman Kodak Company used to have an advertising slogan: 'You press the button, we do the rest', thereby encouraging amongst its customers a somewhat unthinking approach to photography. The hand-held camera and the roll-film revolutionised the medium in the late 19th century and made photography available to the masses and if Kodak did the processing, the 'photographer' didn't have to know anything about that either. He was given the illusion of being a photographer – an *auteur* – by just pressing the button. Power without responsibility.

Technical advances in photography during the 20th century have encouraged this attitude even more, together with another – worship of sophisticated gadgetry. Simpler and more efficient cameras and improved materials should have freed the photographer to consider and investigate *what* is produced, rather than *how* it is produced. But attempts to seriously evaluate a photograph can be complicated and frequently inconclusive. A personal and serious examination of photographic imagery and the medium in general, is rarely undertaken by photographers.

Most camera owners are just that, relying for their reputation as photographers on the possession of easily valued equipment; rather than hard to evaluate judgements of their ability to make pictures with that equipment.

The power of the medium to inform and reveal, whether publicly or privately, cannot be overestimated. But is our knowledge of the functional, let alone the artistic, use of photography good enough? Most of us see scores of photographs each day but do we bother to look at even *one*, to try and find out what it 'says'? The intense critical scrutiny and the frequent rigorous debates which take place in the other arts must surely be worthy of emulation by photographers. The dismissive attitude many people have towards photography comes through ignorance, rather than prejudice. This is understandable if you consider that there are very few specific histories of photography and that photography rarely features in general history books.

But photography is an essential part of modern life. Tens of thousands of manufacturers and service industries throughout the world use, or are dependent on it, so the effect it has on our civilisation is enormous. In 1980 it was estimated that 60% of households in the UK owned a camera, while for the USA the figure was 80% and in Japan, 90%. In 1970, it was estimated that amateurs in Britain alone took 600 million photographs and bought 1,200,000 new cameras. By the late 1970s, just in North America, 750,000 photographs were taken every hour! Most of these pictures were taken, no doubt, by 'holiday-snappers', rather than by professional photographers or artists. But even the untutored amateur can be a serious photographer, assiduously reflecting his life and culture – perhaps, more powerfully than most professionals.

There is something very democratic about black and white photography: everybody can make a photographic image (even people without sight), everything can be reduced or enlarged to the same size, and everything photographed becomes part of the same monochromatic scale. But perhaps its lack of mystique obscures its inherent qualities for most people. Its potential as a vehicle for expression is rarely realised because of its simplicity. We use a camera, but do not know what photography is. We look at photographs, but we do not *see* them.

During most of the history of photography there seem to have been two main camps – one that exploits the medium's verisimilitude (the largest camp), and the other that believes a photograph can transcend the information it contains. One is no *better* than the other – they are just motivated by different approaches. Both need the technical ability to produce the picture wanted, and both introduce other difficulties. The more you find out about photography the more you realise that the photographer has to grapple with philosophical, ethical and moral questions, as well as with technical problems; and some of these questions are debated in the book.

Photography suffers from the fact that its multifarious facets can be conveniently categorised into neat compartments. This is usually done by way of subject (i.e. the objects in front of the camera). What is more relevant – and, one hopes, more illuminating – is the *approach* taken to the subject matter, both visually and intellectually. As photographers have to point their cameras at things that actually exist, you have a marvellous opportunity to interpret the world for yourself rather than represent the ideas and prejudices of others.

You will inevitably be influenced by other people's methods and ideas, but eventually a personal mode of expression and communication emerges. The sheer ubiquity of the medium should not put you off trying to come to grips with it in your own individual way. Although it is very helpful – for a serious study of the medium – to be conversant with various photographic *genres*, 'schools', and movements, you should aim to end up being the controller of your own destiny.

This book is for those who wish to take their photography seriously and beyond the 'holiday-snap' stage. It is divided into two parts. Chapters 1–4 concentrate on many of the basic aspects of photographic image-making and practice: how the camera sees; how to read photographs; how to express yourself and communicate through photography; how and where photography is used in the world today. Chapters 5–9 deal mostly with the different attitudes, current in contemporary photography, concerning the photographer as an observer of events and people; celebrant of nature and man-made objects; documenter of personal emotions; maker of art and artifice; political militant and propagandist. Part I is divided up into specific areas, whereas Part II is much more open-ended. The whole subject of photography is treated questingly, rather than definitively. No book on such a topic can give definite answers; it can just pose the questions. You, the reader, must seek the solutions, your own personal ones.

The photographs have been selected to complement the points in the text. Although they function as illustrations, they should not be thought of as being subservient to the words. As photographs can, and do, work on more than one level of communication, there is the obvious chance that you may read something completely different into many of the illustrations. Good! It is impossible to prove anything *conclusively* in photography, other than that a photograph is the result of the action of light falling on sensitive two-dimensional material.

This book is confined to monochrome photography – not out of prejudice, but because many of the 'basics' concerning photographic image-making, presentation and practice are common to both colour *and* black and white photography. It must be said though that matters relating to the nature of colour and colour photography are distinctly different and the subject should have a whole book devoted to it.

The book deals primarily with approaches to photography that are done for their own sake, in order to inform and/or entertain, rather than to sell a product or service. This does not mean to say that a great deal of the work coming out of advertising studios and other directly functional establishments is photographically unimportant – quite the reverse. However, much of it stems from a complex combination of account executives, graphic designers, art directors, visualisers and, of course, clients, all metaphorically and often literally looking over the photographer's shoulders. The final image is most often as much a product of the skills of others as it is of the photographer. So it is difficult, and often unrewarding, to disentangle the web of visions and motives.

Photography is about communicating ideas and experience as well as information. The camera anchors you to a specific place, or to an idea, which makes it a marvellous tool for exploring, observing and re-presenting both the *external* world and our *internal* reactions to it. In my opinion, no other medium can do these things as well as photography can.

Paul Hill

The Photographers' Place,
Bradbourne, Ashbourne,
Derbyshire, England.

This classic Henri Cartier-Bresson photograph shows most graphically how the camera can 'freeze' movement. Taken in Paris in 1932, only a few years after the 35 mm miniature camera first came onto the market, it is a perfect example of Cartier-Bresson's 'decisive moment' theory, which he describes as 'the recognition of a fact, in a fraction of a second, and the rigorous arrangement of the forms, visually perceived, which gave to that fact expression and significance'

1

SEEING AND THINKING PHOTOGRAPHICALLY

'We see nothing till we truly understand it.' *John Constable (English landscape painter)*

Reading photographs

Photographs surround us nearly all the time, but we rarely consider that they may have to be read closely before they can be understood. The medium's ubiquity does not mean that it is a successful universal communicator – a sort of visual Esperanto – either. Despite what we are often told, photographs do not 'speak for themselves'. Photography should be considered as a language which means that its grammar and its syntax have to be learnt before the medium can be fully exploited by the photographer.

Our ability and means of communication and understanding has a direct relationship to our cultural, social and eductional background and these circumstances inevitably affect us when looking at our own, and other photographers' work. It is also inevitable that you are going to be influenced most of all – as a photographer – by existing photographs that you have seen. This unfortunately, can often lead to the frustrating feeling that 'it's all been done before' – but it hasn't by you, and that is an important thing to remember.

There is also a tendency to relate a photograph to your own experiences but this is true of most things, not just photography. For example, a photograph of the inside of an artery or an intestine will look like a mine or a road tunnel to the uninitiated, not the inside of a part of the human body.

Pre-visualisation and camera vision

Seeing and thinking *photographically* is different from our normal visual and intellectual process. The photographer soon learns that the camera provides a view of the world unlike the one produced by the human optical system. It is, therefore, imperative to become familiar with how a camera *sees*.

When you take a photograph, one of the things you do is *still* a moment of time and a segment of space in front of the lens. The act of 'stilling' is worth further consideration.

Most of us have had to sit still and sketch something at one time, or other, in our lives, usually in the art class at school. The result may not always have conformed to the teacher's idea of good draughtmanship, but the discipline of 'stilling' yourself for a length of time to look closely at an object, whether it be a vase of flowers or a building, almost certainly has a beneficial effect. You were probably not aware of it, but you were analysing the *structure* of the object and the effect *light* was having on it. You were also *making marks* on a piece of paper. This, in a very general sense, is what you do when making photographs. Once the subject has been chosen, the orchestration of the elements that make it up onto a piece of film is the next step, in photography as well as in drawing.

Cameras, of course, have the capacity to 'freeze' time and movement. But even if you are aiming for that candid 'slice-of-life' picture, you have to be aware of *what* you are including in the photograph, via the viewfinder. When you place the camera on a tripod, the process of making photographs takes on a more contemplative 'still' air. Most people adopt an intuitively, instantaneous approach, however, and this tends to delay the contemplation of the subject and the composition until after the camera has automatically 'stilled' the situation. The close examination of the image takes place during the viewing of the negatives and the contact sheet. This is referred to as *post-visualisation*.

Camera formats

The camera you use has a direct effect on the way you make pictures, so it is important to get experience with the different sorts of cameras as soon as possible before deciding which one suits your purposes – and your bank balance.

Two separate features influence the look of the photographs. The size of film determines how smooth and how detailed is the image; though, of course, this too is influenced by the film type, by processing variations and so on. The size of the image also determines the size of the camera, and thus defines its portability and the ease with which it can be used quickly in confined conditions and so on. The film size also introduces another consideration. All other things being equal, the smaller the film the easier it is to make the camera work well in very dull conditions. This is why 35 mm is virtually the universal choice for photo-recordings and candid photography. Modern emulsions and high quality optics allow 35 mm cameras to be used for virtually all types of photography, producing adequately sharp and detailed images under most conditions.

The other major camera feature which affects the way you see the subject, is the viewing system. There are, basically, four types used by serious photographers today; the separate viewfinder, usually with a coupled rangefinder; the single lens reflex (SLR); the twin lens reflex; and the view camera. Cameras with a separate viewfinder are small, light and quiet to use. Those with a *coupled rangefinder* are quick to focus, and the range of lenses offered for interchangeable lens models is usually adequate for most photographers. The main disadvantage is that the tiny image in the

tunnel-like viewfinder tends to discourage the uninitiated from examining the whole composition rather than concentrating on what he regards as the important subject. Most separate viewfinder cameras use 35 mm film, or the smaller snapshot formats.

The most popular configuration – for professionals and amateurs alike – is the *SLR*. The SLR uses a mirror to focus the image that will fall on the film on a horizontal viewing screen. Most models are fitted with a pentaprism viewfinder which gives eye level viewing. The effect is that photographs are taken 'looking straight through the camera', in most cases with the photographer standing erect. The viewing image is larger and more picture-like than that of a separate viewfinder camera, and with a little experience, it is fairly simple to look at the whole composition on the screen. Most SLRs take 35 mm film, and have available an enormous range of lenses and accessories, so that each picture can be composed in the viewfinder to make full use of the comparatively small film area. Those offering bigger images on size 120 film are also popular with serious image-makers. Most of these, and some of the 35 mm models, can be used without the eye-level pentaprism viewing attachment. The picture is then seen and composed directly on the viewing screen, which some photographers find easier. In this configuration, single lens reflexes are much like twin lens reflexes to use. Most *twin lens reflex* cameras take size 120 film. These cameras use one lens to view and focus, and an identical lens forming a similar image on the film to take the picture. Such cameras are almost always held at waist or chest level, producing a slightly different view of the scene.

View cameras (also called large format or plate cameras) use cut (or sheet) film (most 5×4 in) and also have a ground-glass screen. They are bulkier than the other three cameras and are usually used with a tripod. The image on the ground-glass screen is, however, upside down. Extraneous light is usually kept off the ground-glass screen by means of a dark cloth under which the photographer views and focuses.

It must be obvious that a view camera is virtually no good for candid work, but scores heavily over 35 mm cameras if you want fine-detailed, minimum-grain images. A good compromise if you want the latter but without the restrictions of a view camera, is a camera that takes 120 film and produces either 6×6 cm, 6×7 cm or 6×9 cm size negatives.

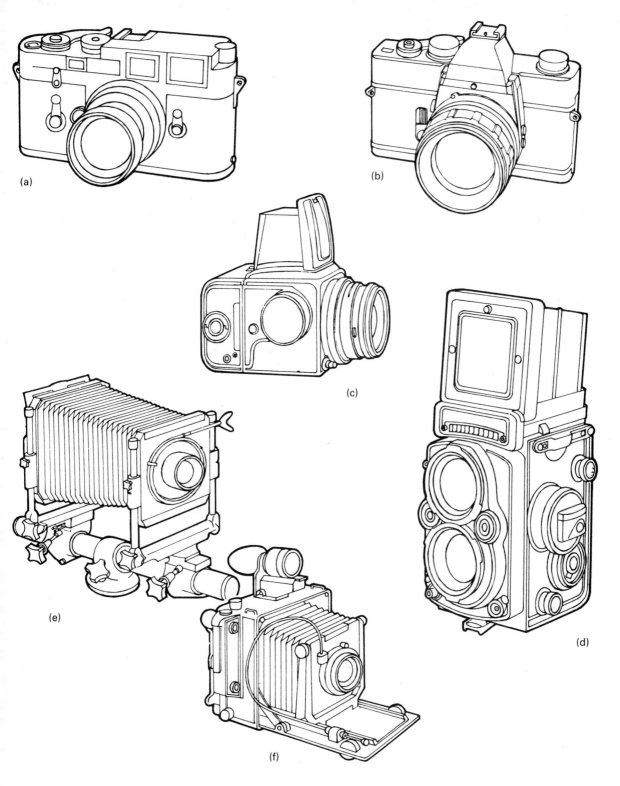

Typical camera formats: (a) 35 mm rangefinder camera with interchangeable lens; (b) 35 mm single lens pentaprism reflex; (c) 120 film single lens reflex; (d) twin lens reflex with fixed lenses; (e) monorail view camera; (f) folding baseboard view camera

The frame

Photography is a very subjective medium despite the apparently objective way it represents what is before the camera. The photographer, after all, controls when the exposure is made, how much light to allow onto the film and – most important-ly – what is included in the picture. The latter is defined by what you frame within the perimeters of the viewfinder, or ground-glass screen.

It might prove an interesting exercise to hold a picture frame out in front of you. Then, imagine that everything you have framed is in monochrome and flat. That is the sort of trans-position you have to make when taking photo-graphs. But what happens outside the frame may be important too. Once the photograph has been taken, however, you can only speculate upon that. Similarly, the viewer may have to ponder some-

times on what the photographer leads him to believe is happening *in* the picture. Your reading of a photograph is usually governed by what you *want* to see in it. In other words, what your cultural and education background dictates is 'there'.

It is important to remember that the photographer cannot photograph what is NOT there.

Photographers can never foretell what other people will make of their images, but they have to be conscious of what they are doing – and the effects their photographs can have. Remember that the photographer can choose which part of the world to 'freeze' for ever, whether it be the expression on a person's face, or a certain section of a particular landscape. This is a great responsibility especially when the results are for public consumption.

Lenses and angles

The frame gives a discipline to work within, but it should not intimidate. To achieve greater freedom of vision, try using different lenses. If you want a wider field of vision, try a wider angled lens; if you want to isolate or compress things in the middle, or far, distance, experiment with a lens that has a longer focal length. Even a standard lens (usually 50 mm on a 35 mm camera) can escape its seeming 'conservatism' if you shoot from different angles of view. Take pictures looking up, looking down. Don't put the camera to your eye all the time. Put it on the ground, hold it above your head. There is no law which says that the world should be seen from a level between five and six feet above the ground.

What is happening beyond the camera's viewfinder can only be guessed at. Who, or what, is the person with the shopping bag rushing away from? Maybe it is just a shopper passing by, or maybe the whole exercise has been staged by the photographer? The frame is the constant factor you have to come to terms with as a picture-maker (Paul Hill)

6

If you want to widen your field of vision, you should use a wide-angle lens. Amongst other things, it gives the picture a feeling of space and depth. This 21 mm lens shot (on a 35 mm camera) enhances the strange spectacle of Cumberland wrestling (at Grasmere), by including the majestic sweep of the surrounding Lakeland mountains as well. A normal lens cannot achieve the dramatic optical effect of the wide-angle. Ultra wide-angle lenses can distort hideously, but if carefully used they can greatly enhance a photograph (Paul Hill)

In order to include as much information in the viewfinder as possible, you can use a telephoto lens. In this picture, taken near Birmingham, there are factories as far as the eye can see. Even so, pockets of land turned into small playing fields can be 'picked out' despite the complex information in the photograph. The 180 mm lens (on a 35 mm camera) used here appears to 'stack' the factories on top of each other (Paul Hill)

8

Taking photographs whilst pointing the camera up or down can produce some interesting results. Here the camera was placed at the same level as the River Derwent at Belper by dangling it over the embankment (as you can see from the end of the fishing rod on the left of the picture). Unless you have a waist-level viewfinder, you have to guess what is in the shot (Paul Hill). The lower picture shows the use of a high vantage point. In this case the photograph was taken from a window of a high-rise building (Richard Sadler)

Tones

In black and white photography, all things become monochromatic tones residing in the same plane. Actual colour and space do not exist. The camera can only record the *light* reflected off the subject matter that the photographer has framed. In a photograph, the separation of the tones – these are grey, not black and white – results from the varying intensities of reflected light off the different objects in the picture. Real colours are not converted by the photographic process into some special grey code. You can see this when you photograph two differently coloured objects that your meter tells you reflect *exactly* the same amount of light. In a *photograph* these two objects will be tonally identical. The reason for this is that your exposure meter is calibrated to read everything as a mid-grey. The photographer has to decide what tones the objects in the photograph will be – another subjective decision.

In black and white photography reflected light is translated into monochrome tones and a subject is defined by the amount of light it reflects onto the photographic film. The puddle of water, the painted white arrow and the wet tyre marks, are the same tone (the tyre marks could easily be mistaken for painted lines), although they are very different objects in actuality (Paul Hill)

'Flattening' the 3D world

The camera frame gives the illusion of being a window through which the photographer views the three-dimensional world. But negatives and prints are flat – two-dimensional. In a photograph, the clouds, the horizon, the ground are all on the same plane. Our perceptual faculties can, of course, make three-dimensional sense of this spacial disparity when looking at a print. When taking the shot you must be conscious that the objects in the picture are flat shapes and you are responsible for the placement of these shapes within the frame. By changing your angle of view you can manoeuvre these forms around the frame almost as if they were cut-outs.

A photograph brings everything in front of the camera onto the same plane. The 'flattening' of the three dimensional world can be exploited by appearing to place objects in the distance onto objects in the foreground. This photograph of the cow 'standing' on the traffic sign was carefully engineered by John Charity, who positioned himself, and his camera, in such a way as to bring the cow and the sign together. A single lens reflex camera is most useful for this type of precisely composed picture as it eliminates parallax

Shadows and light reflected off a shopping centre floor in Birmingham may seem rather uninteresting, but the ephemeral and evanescent are just as 'concrete' as mountains or buildings to the camera. Shadows can hint at the fearful and mysterious, or they can make interesting graphic shapes, but their 'reality' in image-making cannot be denied (Paul Hill)

Translation of the objects in your photographs (this can include evanescent objects like shadows and clouds) into shapes and tones does not come easily but it can be developed with practice.

Illusion

A good example of how totally unconnected objects (shapes) can appear to exist on the same plane is the classic photographic 'mistake' – the human head that has a tree or lampost growing out of it. Most people are aware of this apparent compositional *faux pas*, but few photographers use it to their advantage. There are no rules that say you should not give this illusion of strange things growing out of people's heads. The photographic print presents an illusion anyway and is only, after all, a two-dimensional representation of reality.

Photography has always been a powerful vehicle for visual illusion. Here tree trunks appear to grow out of metal fencing posts to give the appearance of being continuous objects (John Charity)

Dark tones against dark tones tend to merge together, especially in poorly lit places. The boy on the right was wearing dark blue trousers and as the bedhead was black, the two are indistinguishable. His brown sweater merges into his shadow on the wall too. The boy on the left was wearing clothing that reflected more light, so his form can be clearly seen. Even his right arm, which is in shadow, can be made out because it is being held against a light background (Paul Hill)

Light tones against light tones also merge together. The horse's hindquarters are light-coloured and disappear into the white and yellow painted caravan behind it. This can be avoided by trying to get the horse against a darker background, but by the time you have done this, the picture you wanted (i.e. the two horse dealers talking together) may no longer be possible to take! (Paul Hill)

The focal point

When you compose a photograph it is usual to concentrate on a focal point, often a figure or some significant form you want to be the main subject of the picture. This focal point becomes distinguished from the background because the brain always tries to organise and make sense of the visual disorder in front of it. But just because you have isolated the form (which could be a small part of the picture) in your mind does not mean that this will be obvious in the final photograph. At this point consider what is happening in the other parts of the viewfinder. Remember that your picture-plane includes the background as well.

Its intrusion may not be obvious to the human optical system, but in a photographic print the tones that make it up may contain visual 'traps' that our eyes have difficulty in escaping. This may affect the reading of the picture so much that it alters the scene completely. For example, if a dark subject merges into the dark tones of the background it will be lost, and vice versa with light subjects and light backgrounds. Of course, you may be able to 'save' the situation in the darkroom by manipulating the tones when printing, but if the tones of the subject and the background are identical this is very difficult. Anyway, why make hard work for yourself? When making an exposure always try and imagine the resulting print in your mind's eye. By doing this you can avoid problems later.

One of the best ways to isolate your focal point is to place it in the centre of the frame. The couple embracing here in a city park during a rain shower stand out despite the quantity of other information because of their position in the middle of the frame. We tend to read photographs from the centre outwards, rather than from one side to the other as we do when reading sentences (Paul Hill)

Metaphors and symbols

Just as writers use descriptive adjectives and similes to express their reaction to things, so photographers communicate their feelings by the way they photograph the world around them. But with photography the metaphor is not always clear. Images do not convey meaning with the same precision that words do. By photographing a building or a tree, can you show *more* than a building or a tree? On the surface it would appear not, but just as a photograph of a face can reveal the identity of an individual more clearly than a full length shot, it may be possible for a *close-up* detail of a building, or a tree, to express more than a picture of the whole. The 'substance' of an object can be conveyed most strongly by moving closer-in until there is almost a tactile relationship between the photographer and the subject. The close-up abstracts by 'cutting away' the extraneous information through careful framing. You may want to take a close-up photograph of an institution building to convey monumentality or coldness. With the detail of a gnarled tree you may wish to express delicate sensuality or painful

These two photographs, by Raymond Moore, show what a subtle effect small, light shapes against a dark background and small, dark forms on a light surface can give. A herd of remarkably arranged cows in a field, and clods of ploughed earth peeping through a blanket of snow, are the unlikely visual highlights in these two fascinating images

Close-ups of small sections of large objects can often reveal more than a photograph of the entire object. This precisely framed and immaculately executed picture by Ralph Gibson not only symbolises the monumentality of the building (of which it is but a small part), but it also gives an almost tactile impression of the texture of the stone of which the building is made

17

This tree appears to be lacerated but only a small detail of it is visible – the section the photographer wants *us to see. This image is from a series by John Blakemore called* Wounds on Trees. *But the metaphoric intention seems obvious, even if we did not know what the series was called*

convulsions. A caption or title will help direct the viewer to an understanding of your metaphoric intent. You should, however, aim to express the mood or symbolism visually by careful use of exposure, juxtaposition of objects and lighting.

It is *possible* for close-ups to symbolise something more than what is actually recorded on the film. In photography, the objects become *symbols*, because a symbol is a visible sign that represents, or typifies, something else. This is a reasonable description of what the process of photography does – the photographic image of a tree is *not* the tree but a symbol (or sign) for it. But, in addition, if the picture shows a tree isolated in a flat landscape, it could also be said that the tree symbolises something else – perhaps 'loneliness'. A photograph of a flag flying over a public building could symbolise patriotism and national sovereignty to you, but a picture of a model wearing a bikini made up from a national flag would elicit a quite different response.

Juxtapositioning

Another powerful way to express feelings or opinions in photography is by juxtaposing objects and elements within the picture. Dark tones, like shadows, against light backgrounds can evoke mystery and fearfulness. Light and dark can represent good and evil, and so on. Juxtaposition can also heighten the incongruity and absurdity that is apparent in certain situations.

When you juxtapose dark shapes against light ones, you may achieve more than an interesting composition, or graphic exercise. Black traditionally symbolises evil and the feared unknown and white usually signifies goodness and purity. Here the anonymous black figure has a strange shape and appears sinister and unreal, especially when set against an idyllic snow-covered landscape (Paul Hill)

18

Juxtapositioning is one of the most powerful devices used in photography. The pure white swan floating amongst the dirt and flotsam of this Welsh pool emphasises the effect such indiscriminate dumping of rubbish can have on a beautiful landscape. The way that the photographer, David Hurn, has placed the swan in the frame (he relies on the light tones of the bird, rather than size, to make us very aware of it) prevents the picture from being compositionally 'safe' and conventional

'Accidents' can produce creative breakthroughs both in science and the arts. Many photographers discovered that using electronic flash and a slow, unsynchronised, shutter speed produced 'ghosting' in their pictures. This was because the subject either moved during the exposure, or the photographer did, or both. The cat here appears to be casting a shadow against the sky, which looks like a theatrical backdrop (Paul Erik Veigaard)

Being prepared

Care in *pre-visualising* can save hours of needless work in the darkroom. Of course there is a danger in being over-precise when shooting, especially if you want to follow a more flexible, experimental approach. But even in this type of work you need to analyse what you are doing carefully if you want to repeat the effect of an 'accidental' shot.

It cannot be emphasised too strongly that a great deal of practice is necessary to get the results you want. If you use a hand-camera, handle it as much as you can, whether there is a film in it or not. Get used to the viewfinder, the focusing, the aperture ring, even at times when you are not taking pictures. Practice makes musicians instinctively know how to get the notes they want from their instruments and photographers should aim to be equally sure-fingered.

A continuous awareness of *light* is vital in photography. When you go into a room judge how the light is falling, estimate the light reading (confirm this with your exposure meter later) and assess the probable photographic tones and shapes of whatever you look at. You should try to heighten your awareness all the time of what is going on around you, of your own reactions and feelings towards people, things, and events.

Try and master the basic photographic techniques as quickly as possible because this leads to more control and understanding of the medium. Do not blame the mechanics and materials if you are not getting the results you want. If there are problems find out what is going wrong; try and understand what you are doing with photography – and what it is doing to you. Most of the answers will become apparent at the next stage: *post-visualisation.*

Another photographic phenomenon is the mist-like effect you can achieve by using a very slow shutter speed while photographing movement, such as waves crashing on rocks. In this picture the 'whale-like' rocks have been isolated by the photographically induced fog (John Blakemore)

Negatives can give you more technical information about your photographs than your contact sheet after you have learnt to read them. As you can see the 'contact' of frame 16 gives no idea of the wealth of information that is contained in the upper half of the photograph. but it is visible in the negative and, therefore, you know that you can bring it out in the enlargement (Paul Hill)

22

2

AFTER THE SHUTTER IS PRESSED

The negative

As stated earlier, you cannot photograph what is not there. Similarly, you cannot print what is *not* in the negative. If the film has been over-, or under-developed, it is almost impossible to obtain good prints from it. There are several ways of salvaging a bad negative, but making silk purses out of silk is always preferable to making them out of sow's ears!

'Reading' negatives is as important in the photographic process as translating the three-dimensional world into two-dimensions and col-

ours into monochromatic tones. With practice it does not take too long to instantaneously convert the negative into a *positive* in your mind's eye. It soon becomes second nature.

Just remember that the darkest ('densest') parts of each negative are rendered as lightest ('highlights') in the positive print. This includes areas such as the sky, snow, light coloured buildings and blond hair. Conversely, the more transparent ('thinner') parts of the negative become the dark areas in the print. This includes subjects such

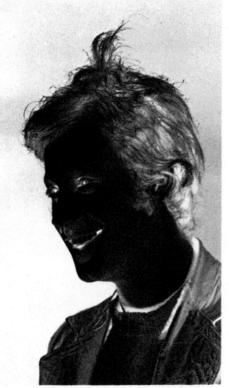 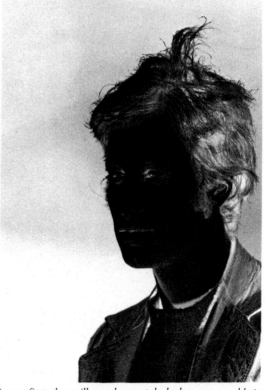

Although things like facial expressions are difficult to discern from negatives at first, they will reveal a great deal when you are able to read them. Just remember that the darker parts of the negative are rendered as light tones in the final print and the lighter parts of the negative are rendered as dark tones

'Blocked-up highlights' (in this case a brightly lit white wall) have been used to isolate the bush (with the photographer's shadow cast on it), the grass, a water spout, and the shadow of another bush. This graphic manipulation also eliminates the frame because the 'highlights', and the base white of the printing paper, are indistinguishable. Many photographers put a funereal black border on their pictures to correct this, but John Mulvany's Self Portrait *emphasises the frame's conventionality by removing it almost altogether*

as shadows, coal, dark coloured buildings and black hair.

After a while you will be able to obtain as much, if not more, information from your negatives as from the positive contact prints of your films. The shapes and tones become easily discernible, although important aspects like facial expressions are much easier to read from contact prints (*contacts*). The negative is the most important technical thing to get 'right' in photography.

24

Over-exposure and/or over-development can 'block up' (make denser) the darker parts of your negatives; so that no light penetrates those parts at the enlarging stage. These featureless white elements in the print can be used as graphic or, in this case, emotive devices (Paul Hill)

This well-known Paul Caponigro photograph is a wonderful example of how photography can abstract tones, forms, and lines, even from an 'ordinary' subject such as this quarry face, and make them into an exciting, almost animated image. Not only is the full range of tones in the grey scale represented in this picture, they are positively celebrated by the photographer

When enlarging your negatives you will find that it is easiest to print those which contain the widest range of tones from the shadow areas through to the highlights. In some cases, you may want a negative that accentuates the highlights, to produce a picture that has a particular graphic quality. This effect can be created by overexposure and/or overdevelopment which 'blocks-up' the highlights. This makes the highlights dense in the negative and consequently lighter in the print.

You can also diagnose errors of exposure, camera operation, focusing and depth of field by closely examining your negatives on a light box, or projected by an enlarger.

Often strange things appear in photographs that you could have sworn were not there when you took them – probably because you were concentrating on other things when you pressed the shutter. A hand clasping an ice cream comes out of the wall on the left in this picture, taken in Scarborough, by Tony Ray-Jones. As an ever-alert professional photographer, he obviously noticed this strange event, but many people would not see such oddities if they were concentrating on the central area of the viewfinder

The same sort of thing is evident in this photograph of a street scene, by Harry Callahan, where the reflected television picture of a pretty girl is apparently floating over the sidewalk

Contact prints

When you make an exposure you are attempting to 'capture' an image that makes some sense out of the welter of information in front of you. No matter how careful you are there are bound to be a great many unknown quantities in your pictures. Your success or failure begins to become evident when you read your *contacts*. Just as you had to make a choice of what to photograph, so you have to select from the contact sheet the images that correspond most accurately to your intentions.

The first shot is rarely the best as your concentration usually improves as you warm to your task, and your awareness is heightened. Contacts of rollfilms are a particular accurate reflection of your working methods and experiences, as well as being a record of the exposures made. They provide visual narratives of your adventures and achievements. In fact, many photographers make their contact sheets their diaries. They become a continuing souvenir of places, people and events which will be interesting to look back upon in years to come.

Ambiguity

One of the first things that strikes you when looking closely at photographs is the ambiguity of the medium. Some objects appear completely different to what you know they are in reality. For example, people reflected in a furniture shop window can appear to be walking on a sofa; the strange play of light on the face of a kind old lady can turn her into a hideous crone.

It is very easy to miss these things at the time, especially if your eye was concentrating on other compositional features, or you were eagerly following an event or incident which was your main subject. Remember that *a photograph shows what the camera records on film NOT what the photographer thought he or she saw.*

Enlarging

Post-visualisation should not only make you aware of these phenomena but help you to deal with them. If you have included elements in your photograph that you do not want in the final picture, it is possible to eradicate or 'hide' them at the *printing* stage. Firstly, by *cropping* them out through manoeuvring your masking-frame under the enlarger or secondly, by darkening or lighten-

ing the objects ('burning' and 'dodging') so that they disappear into the background. Unwanted elements can also include scratches, out-of-focus foregrounds and other mistakes as well as the kind of visual 'traps' mentioned earlier.

The more you become involved in photography the more you realise that the photographic print is an event and experience in itself, not necessarily just a record of what was happening in front of the camera. The photograph should not be expected to mirror truth because 'truth' in visual terms is always subjective.

'The camera never lies' is one of those sayings that should be buried and forgotten with 'You press the button, we do the rest'! You must look at what is in the negative and in the print and deal with that, rather than try to reconstruct your mind's eye's vision of what you thought was there

Sometimes the full frame of the negative contains more than you want in the final print. This photograph also appears on page 19 but that version had been cropped to exclude the telephone wire in order to make the black form more prominent within the perimeter of the print. The final version of this image was exposed to render the coat much darker than it would be normally. This was done to accentuate the two-dimensionality of the black form (Paul Hill)

in actuality. It is important to try and find out, for instance, why the print does not contain the essence of that person, event, or thing you thought you had captured when you pressed the shutter. When you make photographs you are also in a continuum of events affected by all kinds of external *and* internal factors, so you must try and eliminate all extraneous things from your mind and concentrate on the image that you want in the print.

The print

The print is the final stage in the production of the photograph. It is the means of showing your view of the world to others; but the communication will not take place if your printing lets you down. What you 'saw' at the moment of exposure and what you have 'read' in your negative *must* be transmitted through the prints.

In printing you have to control light (through the enlarger lens) in the same way you do when exposing a negative in the camera. This can affect the tones in your prints, as can the contrast of the paper you use. The quality of the photographic paper you choose is most important. If you want to exhibit your work, or just show it to friends, most professional photographers would advise you to use fibre-based paper because of its 'natural' and stable surface. But if the work is to be reproduced in a newspaper, for example, the recently introduced plastic or resin-coated paper would do – although it is archivally unstable. The kind of tones in reproduction will be different from those in your original prints anyway, as the mechanical printing process involves metal plates and ink and not light-sensitive photographic emulsion with all its tonal subtleties. Plastic papers can be very convenient to use and are very fast to process – an important factor in commercial photography. They can also be useful for making contacts and work-prints.

A theme

After a while you will notice that certain features keep repeating themselves in your photographic work. Perhaps you often shoot things from the same angle, or from the same distance. Perhaps you photograph similar types of individuals, events or places. It could be that the same mood or atmosphere occurs time and again in your images; or similar shapes and forms become repeating motifs. Try to discern from your photographs

Although this may appear to be a successful fully-tonal print, with hardly any featureless white – or black – tones, there is a lack of contrast in the tones. This is called a 'flat' print

In order to obtain more contrast in the print, a 'harder' grade of printing paper nearly always must be used. Although this increases the evidence of 'grain' in the negative, the light tones will go lighter, and the dark tones will go darker

29

what may be an emergent *theme*. A theme may have more to do with the *way* you photograph than with *what* you photograph. In other words, the way you *see* the world – your individual vision.

Your ideas and concerns, if focused on a particular subject, will be like a piece of grit in an oyster around which your work will begin to grow. Eventually a coherent body of work will possibly emerge. But it takes time for a pearl to form – and not every oyster produces one. However, beware of superficial success and easy re-

These two photographs come from a sequence, called Light, *which aimed to convey the many forms in which light manifests itself – even in the most ordinary of situations. Visually dramatic evidence of light can be found in places like high-street shopping arcades. Reflected neon lighting can appear to be like a white laser beam penetrating a marble wall or a shop window dummy. Although the theme was 'light', these two images show how subsidiary concerns can reinforce the cohesive quality of the sequence, and thereby add extra elements to it (Paul Hill)*

sults. You may produce a series of photographs that are slick imitations of current fads and fashions; if so, do not stay at this unavoidable imitative stage for too long. Precociousness is no substitute for depth.

Sequencing prints

Photographs are signs and symbols for ideas, and by conscious and careful arrangement – sequencing – they can convey specific ideas. The order and positioning of your prints when displayed – either on a wall or in a publication – are crucial to the communication of the *statement* you are making through your work. Although the statement may be made up of many different elements (including single prints that can also work on their own), the sequence should have an overall unity and effect, whether it is a realistic or abstract subject. Unity can be achieved by repetition of shapes and tones as well as by the use of recurrent symbols or objects. The ephemeral and the solid are equally strongly portrayed by the camera.

The shape of the print can also be a repeating motif in a sequence, as this diamond-shaped picture, from Kenneth Baird's Horizon Series I, *clearly demonstrates. The series has, of course, other things than an unusual format to commend it too*

Sentimental and allegorical paintings like this pre-Raphaelite work by P.H. Calderon called Broken Vows, *exemplify the type of art that influenced many Victorian photographers (Courtesy Tate Gallery)*

3

ART AND COMMUNICATION

What is art?

The eminent art historian, Professor Ernst Gombrich wrote: 'There is no such thing as Art – there are only artists'. The French painter, Debuffet, said of art: 'Its best moments are when it forgets what it is called'. Although photography is a unique medium, it has always been compared with the more autographic arts. Even today, many people are still concerned by the question of whether photography is art, or not.

Early developments

The concept of photographic representation was appreciated hundreds of years before the process of photography was discovered. The development of the theory of perspective in the 15th century gave drawings and paintings the illusion of three-dimensionality in the same way that photographs do. This proved a wonderfully successful technique for the painters who wanted to improve accurate representation. As a result the *camera*

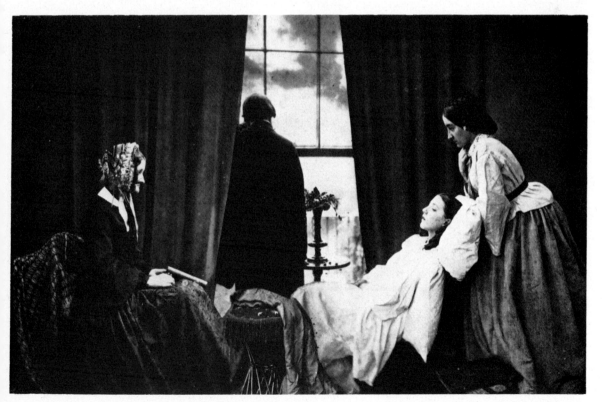

One of the most successful 'artistic' photographers in the 19th century was Henry Peach Robinson, who produced many Salon-acclaimed works that owed much to pre-Raphaelite painting. Although it must be said that many pre-Raphaelites were, ironically, accused of copying photographs in the early 1850s. Robinson 'constructed' his photographs and this famous picture, called Fading Away (1858) was made up of five different negatives and printed in combination. This type of photography, called 'pictorialism', was seen as a passport to artistic respectability and dominated most serious exhibition photography until the First World War (Courtesy Royal Photographic Society)

Blurred 19th century photographs influenced the Impressionist painters and later the continuous-action images made by Etienne Jules Marey (and Eadweard Muybridge) not only heralded the invention of cinematography, but also greatly affected the Post-Impressionist painters and the Futurists. That experimental genius Marcel Duchamp acknowledged the influence that Marey's (photographs) had had on him, particularly in his painting Nude Descending a Staircase, 1912

obscura was used to project a light-reflected image onto a flat surface which could be traced by the artist. The image became sharper when the aperture allowing the light in was smaller or, better still, if the light was focused through a lens.

These devices were particularly popular amongst amateur painters eager to find a quick, foolproof way to emulate the paintings of their professional peers who possessed the accurate draughtmanship and skill that they lacked. But many prominent painters like Canaletto also used

the camera obscura, and so did the scientist and amateur painter, Henry Fox Talbot, the man who invented the negative/positive method of photography that we use today.

Light-sensitive silver salts and an efficient method of permanently fixing the image 'caught' by an improved portable version of the camera obscura produced the early photographs of 140 years ago – and basically the same system produces photographs today.

Influence of photography on art

The invention of photography released painters from their representational role which meant that the more perceptive of them could pursue their investigations into the nature of their medium — the act of painting. Photography had an enormous effect on the artists of the 19th century as it still does today. The Realist painters, like Millet and Courbet, were obviously affected, after all their motto was: 'You cannot paint what you cannot see'. Out-of-focus and blurred photographic images interested the Impressionists (whose first exhibition in 1874 was held in a studio lent to them by Paris photographer, Nadar) as did the capturing of fleeting human gestures and positions, and the unique ways in which the photographic frame crops things. Multiple images and frozen movements were two of the photographic phenomena utilised by Modernist painters in the early 20th century. Photography has been an important factor in the development of Surrealism, Dadaism, and the more recent Photo-Realism and Conceptual movements.

Influence of art on photography

Events like the French Revolution which signified a victory for individual liberty, lent impetus to the growth of personal expression in the arts. The free-thinking artist, whose uncompromising bohemian life-style annoyed the establishment, became the radical's hero.

In Britain, most artists and writers on Victorian art were seeking romantic beauty. Lovingly crafted artefacts became the antidote to galloping industrialisation with its soulless factories, human exploitation and machine-made products. Photographs, however, were made by machines; they could also be mass-produced and unartistic businessmen were getting rich by making them. So, unfortunately, photography got tarred with the brush of utilitarianism — acceptable for the artisan, but anethema to the 'real' artist. As a reaction many photographers copied salon painting — often producing sentimental and allegorical photographs that denied the intrinsic advantages of the medium in order to produce some dubious 'artistic' quality. Consequently there are no photographic heroes in books on the history of art, despite the undoubted power and influence of the medium.

But should photographers worry whether they are elevated into the pantheon of great artists? As one contemporary doyen of the art world (Lawrence Gowing) recently remarked: 'Photography is *more* than Art'. After all, painting can never have that descriptive authenticity inherent in photography. A photograph does reveal something other than imagination and material. The photographer has to deal with the external world, however internal his preoccupations.

Although photographs, like paintings, can be said to be *made* rather than *taken*, the method is very different. A painter constructs his picture rather like an inventive bricklayer whereas a photographer searches for a ready-made scene. The sensuous attraction of coloured oil paints and the comfort of a womb-like studio can be seductive, especially as the end-product is always called Fine Art, which has a long, and mostly honourable history. The search on a grey winter's day for the elusive photographic image that will interest, illuminate, or even excite, can be frustrating, confusing and uncomfortable, by comparison.

Both mediums are affected, however, by the norms of acceptability set by art dealers, critics, editors, graphic designers and so on. The degree to which you are affected by these external influences is up to you.

But do not worry if you feel you have been (obviously) influenced by what is 'in' at the moment — everybody is. Use the experience as a springboard — a point of departure — for more individualistic efforts. You may, however, reject the 'art for art's sake' notion, and prefer to work in the 'real' world inhabited by 'ordinary' people to whom you can better relate. A great deal of modern art nowadays seems to have no functional use and is often elitist and esoteric in nature. Art, after all, cannot exist without man, but physically man can exist without art.

Evidence of the power of individual, or collective, creative expression may be hard to find in the everyday world, but its influence is pervasive — and often feared by those in authority. As Queen Victoria is quoted as saying: 'Beware of artists — you do not know where they have been!'. It can be no coincidence that the free-thinking artist is one of the first to be locked away by dictators in totalitarian states.

Photographers should probably stop trying to seek respectability and status in the art world. Their energies could be more profitably directed towards attempting to make sense of the world, and their place in it.

This two-page spread in Life *news magazine shows how photographers can reflect and interpret an event (in this case the British G* and the vanquished on such occasions. The headline does direct our attention to this interpretation, it is true, but the photographs illu

TORY EXUBERANCE, LABOR WOE

Britons give Eden vote of confidence

Hailing supporters in his home constituency on election night last month, Sir Anthony Eden justifiably wore the exultant expression of a man who has just gambled and won. Only 51 days after he succeeded Sir Winston Churchill in the British prime ministry, Eden risked his government in a general election. The result sent Eden back to 10 Downing Street with a working Conservative majority of 59 seats in the House of Commons, better than three times the margin with which Churchill had to make do for three-and-one-half years. It was, as Eden said, a mandate to "get on with the job" of proving that progressive Conservatism works.

Although the victory was by no means overwhelming, its effect on the feud-racked Labor party was demoralizing. The schism between the moderate Socialists led by Clement Attlee and the fiery radicals led by Aneurin Bevan seemed sure to be deepened as a result of election post-mortems. Now 72, Attlee has probably fought his last general election. As the bad news rolled in, he looked like a man at the end of Socialism's road.

EXULTANT TORIES hail Patricia Hornsby-Smith who won easily in a supposedly marginal district.

BEATEN-DOWN ATTLEE still flaunts campaign rosette at 3:45 a.m., after party's defeat was certain.

SMALL COMFORT is enjoyed by Attlee when his wife congratulates him on his personal re-election.

◄— **HUGE SATISFACTION** overcomes Eden as he beams beneath a board recording own re-election.

on of 1955). The captions identify the people and the situation, but the photographs alone show the elation and sorrow of the victor is happening. We can actually see for ourselves the reaction of the major protagonists (Courtesy of Life magazine ©Time Inc. 1955)

Personal expression

Personal expression, whether in words or pictures, can be very intimate and subjective and consequently communication with other people may often prove difficult. People tend to dislike or fear what they cannot understand, so if a piece of work is inscrutable, antipathy usually results. But you should try to find out why you do not like something before condemning it out of hand. Closely examine the work and try to discern the maker's intention. You will probably learn something. You may not the like the work any more, but at least you may know why. Blind prejudice can be much more dangerous than any artistic movement, as history has proved. Remember, it is by exploring new and exciting possibilities that you develop your creative and intellectual capabilities.

Links with literature

The history of photography's discovery and early development make the rivalry between the new medium and painting understandable. But is photography closer to literature than to painting? Words describe things, as do photographs. This is obvious in reference to objects in front of the camera/observer, but it can be more problematic when the photographer wants to express, rather than show, something. A certain type of descriptive writing in the mid-19th century was called 'a photograph', often perjoratively. A metaphor consisting of words can conjure up a visual image, and a photographic image can also operate as a visual metaphor.

A photograph of a solitary cloud could evoke a similar response as Wordsworth's famous line, 'I wandered lonely as a cloud', if the photographer conveyed that interpretation skilfully. A picture of a cloud which also shows part of a football game, is unlikely to convey the same metaphor! Words are available to us all in the same way as things around us are available to be photographed. Once we have learned the basics of visual grammar we can use the results to communicate and express whatever we want to. A sequence of photographs probably bears a closer relationship to writing than it does to any of the other visual arts.

Narrative flow

The *photo-essay* attempts to convey a sense of narrative through its layout and interrelation of pictures and use of captions, whether the subject

of 'the story' is a person, an event, or a place. But the viewer still has to impose the flow of a story-line on the string of individual images presented. The successful communication of the story is as much a tribute to the perception and imagination of the viewer as to the skill of the photographer.

However animated the scene, a photographic print is always a *still* photograph. Images produced in this way, however, can be contemplated and examined without having to set up a projector and screen or video-tape machinery. The photograph can be explored at leisure for as long as you wish and referred to whenever you like.

The moving image

It may seem strange to compare photography with literature, but it could be considered equally odd to compare photography with film or television. Just because their images are produced by the action of light on sensitive material via a camera does not mean that film-making and TV are similar disciplines to still photography. Moving pictures give a sense of continuity – a narrative – that still photography tries to emulate through the *photo-essay* and the *sequence*, but the illusion of reality is much more successfully achieved in films and television than in 'stills'. Movies capture a semblance of the continuum in which we live, despite the fact that the results are just as artificial as those produced by still photography. Blurred photographs may give the impression of movement but they will always appear to be contriving an effect in comparison with the real sense of movement conveyed in film and television.

Mixed media

Photography, film and television may frequently overlap, but they are nonetheless very different in their application. The choice of medium should be governed by its appropriateness in the context of your ideas. If film, television, or sound can communicate your ideas better than still photography, use them. Stretch photography as far as you want, but do not expect it to do things that it is incapable of. Never be afraid to use a mixture of media to produce the effect you want. But remember if you are too capricious and gimmicky in your use of media, the result may appear superficial. Your intention can be destroyed by too flashy a technique which has little substance or lasting power.

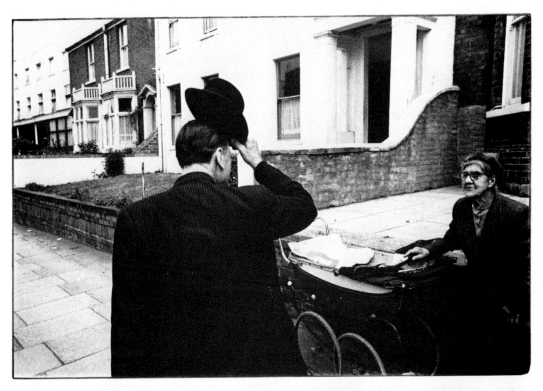

To give a sense of cinematic-like narrative with still photographs, is asking a great deal of the medium. But this can sometimes be achieved by an 'action/reaction' sequence. Here, politician Enoch Powell doffs his hat to a woman supporter, who, in the second picture, eagerly gives her reaction to the gesture to an interested passer-by (Paul Hill)

The blurred effect you can achieve from panning your camera with the action can frequently give the illusion of movement, particularly in sports photography. The blurred legs and background can give an effective impression of speed even though they cannot show 'real' movement as cinema and television can (Paul Hill)

Visual impact

The weird images produced by ultra wide-angle and zoom lenses can give that eye-catching impact so evident in professional photography today. Visual impact is used like a magnet to attract the viewer's attention to the advertiser's product or, in magazine photo-journalism, to the writer's story. Advertising sells 'dreams' as much as journalism sells 'angles' and the camera is a powerful weapon in both their arsenals.

The technical, creative and professional acumen employed by advertising, newspaper and magazine photographers can be awe-inspiring, but it is necessary to decide whether the work contains *more* than a consummate facility with the medium, or the photographic industry's latest technological gimmick. The 'dream-sellers' of advertising and the 'propagandists' of journalism may not always present the *truth* as we understand it, but nevertheless their work gives a great many useful insights into how commerce and society works. A photograph is an illusion of reality and can be exploited by those who wish to 'manipulate' their audience. It may be a cynical point of view but both advertising and journalistic photography reflect the old newspaperman's tongue-in-cheek maxim: 'Never let facts interfere with a good story'.

When you pan the camera with a wide-angle lens, you can create some strange effects which give the picture the sort of visual impact that attracts a viewer. Here the lens appears to be stretching the racing car. This enhances the impression of speed created by the panning. The shadows on the track add an air of strange unreality to the situation (Paul Hill)

There are as many ethical and moral questions to be considered in photography as there are in life, but do not let these problems have an unnecessarily inhibiting effect. The doubts and fears you may have will rarely be resolved by theory — but they may be resolved by the *practice* of photography. As long as your actions do not give rise to unnecessary suffering or offence to 'shoot first, ask questions later' may be the best way to learn photography.

Ritual Indication, near Alton, 1977, *from a series called* Atonements

Titles are an essential part of the work of many photographers whose images appear in art galleries. Thomas Cooper is drawn towards aspects of 'ritual and ceremony' that he finds in the landscape, and he indicates this in the titles he uses

A SOURCE OF THREE INDUSTRIAL RIVERS

A photographer once said: 'There is nothing more mysterious than a fact clearly stated'. This work by Roger Palmer (here much reduced) proves this statement. The text states a fact, but the photograph apparently shows something else – a minimal landscape with not a trace of water in sight. His photograph is geographically correct but it can never confirm the title. Reality and truth reside in the mind, not on pieces of paper

4

HOW PHOTOGRAPHY IS USED

Where do we put photographs?

'This exhibition is not for the public, it's only for one person – it is for you who are here.'

Man Ray (photographer and painter) in an exhibition catalogue.

Images, like sounds, have no intrinsic significance. It is the interpretation put on them by the maker and then by the viewer that gives them meaning.

There are few *rules* to aid the communication between the photographer and the viewing public, just guidelines. People tend to relate to the *content* (subject matter they can recognise) first, and to the composition – *form* – second. We usually see what we want to and not always what is actually there. This has a great deal to do with our cultural and educational background and also to do with the *context* (i.e. galleries, portfolios, books, magazines, newspapers and posters) in which the work is seen. Your reaction, for example, to a 'fine' print in an art gallery, of fungus growing on peeling wallpaper would be different from your reaction to a reproduction of the same print illustrating an article on damp in housing estates.

This difference in interpretation should not be confused with dishonesty. Integrity cannot be a characteristic of photography, but it can be a quality possessed by the photographer. The fungus and the peeling wallpaper are neutral but the way you photograph them and the way you present the photograph is not.

Captions and titles

You should be very aware of the implications of your actions when you put your work on public view of any sort. Photographs do not speak for themselves. You might be quite happy for the viewer to make up his own mind, but if you want him to get your point, you must give a few signposts. This can be achieved by the use of captions and titles and also perhaps by using a complementary text, or even sound.

Captions are usually written to help explain what is going on in the picture and are often quite lengthy. The personalities, the location, the event, the date, and, perhaps, the photographer are identified. This type of captioning is probably most

Photographs as evidence: fungus and damp in a hallway. For Walterton Road Residents' Association

The context in which photographs are seen and used is often a fundamental factor in the understanding of them. A 'fine' print of this photograph of fungus and peeling wallpaper would be similar to many such abstract still-lives that are seen in photographic exhibitions. But it was not taken to be hung on a gallery wall; it was used to prove that damp was badly affecting a housing estate, as we can see from the caption (Philip Wolmuth, North Paddington Community Darkroom) familiar to us as it is used in newspapers and magazines and also in displays of documentary photography.

Titles are usually succinct and often allude to the emotional, or conceptual, source that the photographer has used for the pictures. Whether witty or serious, obvious or obscure, they are either subservient to the image – interesting appendages rather than necessities – or an essential component of each picture.

Very often photographers include a written statement with the pictures explaining their intentions and working methods. This can also contain biographical details and/or an explanation as to how the photographer arrived at the ideas reflected in the work. Sometimes a poem or a piece of prose by a writer will complement the work more successfully than anything the photographer could write himself.

Galleries

Galleries have walls on which pictures can be hung. But the simplistic nature of this description may indicate why so many photographers do not use galleries well. Photogaphers who show their work in galleries for the first time find it difficult to come to terms with the type of space afforded them. Before you can come to terms with galleries

THE MAN WHO INVENTED HIMSELF

Everything that he experienced in his lifetime were his inventions. He invented the moon and the stars and all things visible and invisible. At this moment he is inventing me writing this and you reading this. Yes you too are his invention. Yet if you told him this, he

would deny it. Even though all things that he taught were possible became possible; and all things that he thought were impossible became impossible. He would even invent his own death. and he would never know that he had invented it all.

Supplementary text with photographs can take many forms. In Duane Michals' case, he often writes on the actual print next to the image he has made. He describes emotions and events that are important for him to communicate, but impossible to show in a photograph. Commenting on his frustration at not being able to photograph 'reality', Michals has said: 'I am a reflection photographing other reflections within a reflection'

Galleries come in differing shapes and sizes and there are many other variables. The walls on which the work is hung may also be painted in different ways, thus affecting the 'look' of the show. Lighting systems can vary tremendously and good lighting is essential to present photographs at their best. All these factors – plus image size, and framing – have to be strongly borne in mind when considering the gallery venues for your photographs (Paul Hill)

you will have to consider the appropriateness of walls, frames and so on, for your work and the relevance of your photographs to gallery presentation.

Some galleries are similar to mausoleums, whilst others are like noisy boutiques; but many are in-between – serious, without being forbiddingly solemn. You will have to choose the sort of gallery that best suits your work.

The kind of gallery you are probably most familiar with is the specialist photographic gallery. Many of these are non-profitmaking establishments heavily supported by public funds. Your work in the context of these galleries will be considered with other contemporary photographers' work. It would be advisable to choose the gallery whose philosophy and policy fits in best with your own interests. Some gallery directors have very catholic tastes, whilst others are interested in one particular sort of photography to the exclusion of everything else. Their exhibition policies usually speak for themselves.

Many galleries that normally exhibit paintings, prints and sculptures also show photographs from time to time. In these settings your work will be displayed with the other visual arts and will tend to be compared with them in terms of presence and conceptual rigour. These exhibition areas may be in a municipal museum, art gallery or art centre, or they may be run by an art dealer who can survive only by selling work. The latter type of gallery attempts to attract collectors and is often catering for market requirements.

Exhibition outlets are, however, not confined to those listed above. You can display your photographs in stores, leisure centres, schools, hospitals, or even on board ships if you like! In fact, anywhere where there is a place to show pictures. Where you show should depend on your preferences and the way you want your work to be seen.

One of the best ways to appreciate photographs is to hold them in your hands, so that you can examine and explore them carefully and in comfort. If they are mounted, they can be handled easily too. Prints should be stored in a portfolio box to prevent them being damaged by careless people, or by atmospheric pollution. This attitude to photographs may appear fussy but it reflects a caring and respectful approach to a photographer's work (Paul Hill)

Hanging prints

When investigating exhibition outlets you should also consider the lighting (strong, even illumination is necessary for most photographs), the height of the walls (small prints on huge walls get 'lost' because they probably need an intimate atmosphere), the length of the walls (the sequential development of your prints and how they are hung depends on the length and continuity of the walls) and the publicity (there is little point in working hard to produce an exhibition that nobody sees).

This type of research pays dividends because it indicates what size your prints should be, how you should mount them (the type of mounting card, the dimensions of the window-matts which surround the prints), whether you should frame or not (if you do, the sort of frame – metal, wood or perspex – the type of glass, the fixings), the number of prints to be shown (try to avoid using every exhibition like a retrospective of your 'best' photographs; show the prints that cohere most effectively) and the best print(s) to use for the invitation and/or poster for the show (the choice should reflect the theme or style of the exhibition and have a striking impact).

Portfolios

It is probably easiest to contemplate a photograph by holding a simply mounted print in your hands. You can then explore the image in its 'raw' state without glass and frame and the distractions of a public place. Portfolios of prints presented in this way can be experienced in the comfort of your home, or in the relative tranquillity of a museum archive or library. Most of the time your work will be in portfolio form but you should not confuse a box of loose, dog-eared prints with a portfolio. A portfolio is like a small portable exhibition, cleanly mounted and carefully boxed. If it is acquired by an archive it should be processed for permanence, which means that the prints have to be cleansed of all potentially destructive chemicals and mounted with suitable adhesives on acid-free boards. This sort of conservation is not preciousness, it is just good photographic practice which should mirror the care and concern of the photographer for his medium – and his work.

Publishing and reproduction

Galleries and portfolios are the most effective ways for the public to see your original prints, but it is obviously not the only way they can see photographs. Fortunately, photographs can be reproduced and often on a massive scale, in books, magazines, newspapers and posters.

In the same way that it is flattering to be asked to exhibit in a gallery, it is gratifying to see your photographs in print, especially if your name is by the picture. These reactions are natural and should not be despised. But you should not accept an invitation to exhibit, or be published, out of conceit alone. Hopefully you have something to say in your pictures or in the case of a *commission* be able to do the job successfully!

However, the pitfalls of publishing work in reproduced form are legion. One of the major reasons for advocating caution is that when your work is reproduced, the reproduction is done by others who rarely care as much as you do about your pictures. This means that you are almost always at the mercy of the editors, designers and printers. On many occasions there is excellent co-operation and the results bear this out, but it is often the photographs that suffer. In the same way that a photograph is a representation of actuality, so a reproduced photograph is only a *copy* of the original photographic print – and often a inferior one.

Page 48—Fay Godwin is a photographer who has participated in many book publishing ventures. In Remains of Elmet *(Faber and Faber) she collaborated with the poet Ted Hughes. To bring out the subtleties of the photographs, the printing reproduction had to be of a very high standard. The placement of the image on the page also had to be carefully considered as did the positioning of the lines of the complementary poem. In* Elmet, *the skills of Godwin and Hughes were not subservient to each other – they were partners in the communication of an experience*

Page 49—Self-publishing can be a way of showing your work to a wider public. Brian Griffin produced a monograph without any written material in it – just his photographs, and simple line motifs drawn by Barney Bubbles. But the project was tackled with an appreciation of the sequential relevance of the pictures, and the layout design which is so important in a book was carefully considered. Although these sort of publishing ventures are thought of by many as exercises in vanity, they are nonetheless courageous attempts to defy the 'play-safe' attitude of most commercial publishers

Open To Huge Light

Wind-shepherds
Play the reeds of desolation.

Dragged out of the furnace
They rose and staggered some way.
It was God, they knew.

Now hills bear them through visions
From emptiness to brighter emptiness
With music and with silence.

Startled people look up
With sheeps' heads
Then go on eating.

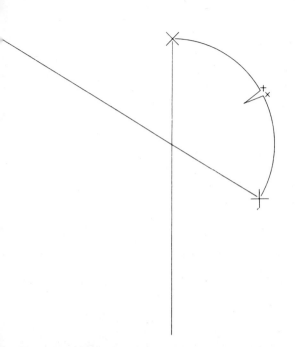

Books

Facsimile reproduction is often attempted in book publishing, but this requires a high level of printing skill and can be very expensive. Publishers of photographic monographs usually make every effort to achieve facsimile reproduction and sometimes the reproductions even improve on the originals! Although good reproduction can be crucial to the success of a book of photographs, the lay-out and sequence of the images are equally important.

As monographs concentrate on the work of one photographer, it is usual to put only one image on a page so that the reader can see each photograph as an individual piece – almost as if it were in a portfolio. The selection of photographs that are to be on facing or alternate pages, the choice of text and typography, the exact placement of the image on each page, and most importantly, the format and size of book, are usually decided by the designer in consultation with the photographer. But if the photographer is only illustrating a book he/she will have very little say in the design and choice of pictures. In fact the photographs may be subservient to the text *and* the design.

Commissions

If you undertake to provide photographic illustrations, establish how the pictures are going to be used and on what basis you are commissioned. The excitement of getting your work published may quickly turn to disappointment if you find that the pictures you strove so hard to make have been insensitively cropped or badly reproduced. Without proper stewardship a potentially excellent showcase for your photography could turn

The sensitivity and compassion displayed by photo-journalists whilst under physical and mental stress has been the hallmark of the best war photographers. Philip Jones-Griffiths took this picture during the Tet Offensive in the Vietnam War, and it shows the plight of the innocent victims of such tragedies. Jones-Griffiths went further than most war photographers, however, and investigated many aspects of the war away from the battlefields in his book Vietnam Inc. *This gave a great deal of background and information that helped explain the war in a way that would have been impossible for his photographs alone to have done*

A 'scoop' may never come a photographer's way because it is more to do with luck and being in the right place at the right time, than with talent. Whatever else I. Russell Sorgi may have done in his life, this picture – Suicide 1942 – is what he will be remembered for. It was a once-in-a-lifetime moment, which even the tragedy of the incident cannot diminish (I. Russell Sorgi, Buffalo Courier)

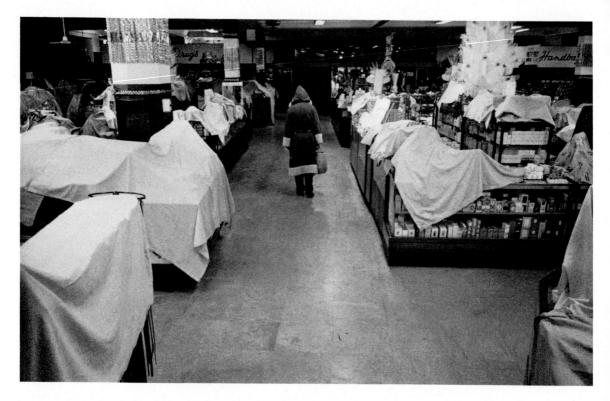

Some newspapers seem only to deal with the more trivial items of news; but even 'serious' newspapers like The Guardian *like to take a light-hearted and bizarre view of the world sometimes. They used this picture on their front page one Christmas to illustrate the seasonal nature of some jobs at that time of the year! (Paul Hill)*

out to be a disaster for your photographic career. It is often a good idea to settle conditions and requirements in writing first, so that both parties know where they stand. Another solution may be to engage the services of a respected literary or photographic agent.

Magazines

The same problem could arise in dealing with magazines, but as periodicals come out regularly you will have a good opportunity to study 'the market' before you enter into any arrangement with them. Always be suspicious of an editor who will not give you any idea of how your photographs will be laid out. This is particularly relevant to photographic magazines who rely on photographs for their raw material. Once they have committed themselves to publishing your work, they *should* treat it with respect; ensuring that it is reproduced to the highest standard their printers are capable of. Having said that, it might be fair to add that the vast majority of publications are not run by philanthropic organisations,

and they can only afford to go as far as the economics allow.

Newspapers and photo-journalism

What is news? There is a humorous definition you may have come across which declares that news is 'when man bites dog, not when dog bites man'.

Drama and gossip are the important main-stays of most popular newspapers, whilst the more 'serious' ones set out to be organs of record and interpreters of important events. Unfortunately, a strong sense of caricature invariably results from popular journalism's treatment of most news items. Stories are also exaggerated, and frequently issues become very black and white. Newspaper photography is bound to be affected by the same ethos. For example, a photograph of a prominent politician delivering a speech will rarely warrant publishing, but if he, or she, slips on a banana skin, it is front-page news.

It could be argued that this kind of photograph reveals the human side of our political leaders but it also demonstrates that trivial incidents often make the most popular pictures. Unfortunately, the search for the bizarre by newspapers often reflects this trivial attitude, and the results can seem laboured and/or predictable.

Newspaper photographers are always on the look-out for an exclusive. Being in the right place at the right time – luck, in other words – is more likely to produce a memorable 'scoop' than the visual talent of the photographer. Many 'scoop' pictues have been taken by local newspaper and agency photographers, who are rarely heard of again. The best news photographers gain their reputation by their consistency, reliability and perseverance – commendable qualities in any profession – and their tenacity is sometimes rewarded by that 'once-in-a-lifetime' shot.

Courage is frequently essential when photo-reporting in potentially explosive areas of the world. But the finest photo-journalists exhibit a sensitivity and compassion that belies their rugged, and ruthless, image. Photographs of the pitiful casualties of war can be much more revealing in human terms than action pictures of shooting and bombing. They have a universal, lasting quality that can demonstrate man's frailty and innocence and at the same time, his capacity for senseless cruelty; the 'human condition' is thus reflected in actual life and death terms.

Although, at any one time, there are many parts of the world that are being destroyed by war or riddled by corruption, most of us are not affected directly by headline dramas. Our involvement with them via the media, is vicarious, even voyeuristic. Newspapers thrive on the fact that whilst the majority of their readers are passive, armchair observers, their reporters are 'out there' risking life and limb in order to bring us 'the real

To interpret important news events in terms of a single image is what newspaper photographers attempt to do in their photographs. The 1970 General Election was dominated by Member of Parliament, Enoch Powell, whose political rhetoric concerning immigration and allied matters caused quite a stir. The boy's bubble of gum seemed to mirror the hyperbole used in many of Powell's speeches, as well as appearing to symbolise the sort of reaction his critics were voicing at the time (Paul Hill)

On distressingly numerous occasions, and with certain types of assignments, it is very easy to slip into one of the visual clichés that a genre throws up. In this case, it is the successful businessman in the foreground amongst the products that have made him rich (Paul Hill)

story behind . . .'. And though the frequently hyperbolic and predictable nature of many photographs used in popular journalism may be embarrassing, a great deal of important and revealing work – which often discloses the flavour of our times better than long, in-depth magazine features – gets through.

When covering events for newspapers (as opposed to magazines), it is important to remember that a picture editor tends to look for 'the picture that tells the story'. If this picture is dramatic as well then it will almost certainly be published. It is unlikely that more than one photograph will be published per story, even though you may have a most interesting series of images.

On many occasions the possibilities for obtaining visually interesting photographs are limited, but it is important to keep searching for that elusive picture. It is usually there somewhere. Lack of time may force you towards the hackneyed image but do not despair. The wide-angle portrait of managing-director-holding-firm's-product-in-front-of-factory, so loved by many photographers and picture editors was thought quite *avante-garde* when it first appeared many years ago.

The predictability of many journalistic jobs, and the lack of time allowed to do them in, often produces a very stylised approach which sets a particular photographer apart from most of his contemporaries. Brian Griffin is one such photographer. He specialises in portraits of people involved with the commercial and the show business world. Here he has taken a back view of the managing director of a book publishing firm, which seems to make the book the subject of the picture, not the man. The arrow at his feet adds an interesting graphic dimension to the photograph

Constant repetition of the same type of assignment tests the most visually ingenious photographer and in an effort to come up with something 'different', exaggeratedly stylistic approaches are sometimes adopted. As a result of this, photographic show-stoppers can emerge that inevitably reveal style rather than 'truth'.

The predictability of a large percentage of newspaper assignments can be dispiriting, but to a photographer the continuous pressure and shortage of time, and the largely diabolical newsprint reproduction can be even more disheartening. Luckily some newspapers have good photographic reproduction and do allow their photographers more freedom and time to exercise their visual talents.

Posters and photo-murals

If a photograph is going to be used as a poster or mural remember that your image – whether in original or reproduction – will be enlarged many more times than normal. Consequently there will be a loss of certain qualities that are in a smaller print. There will be an increase in photographic 'grain' which may give a pleasing pointillist effect, but posters usually depend on size for their impact and are therefore viewed from a distance – increased grain size should not therefore be noticeable. Larger negatives can be used to decrease grain if this is important. The physical constrictions of gallery frames, archival boxes, book pages, magazine lay-outs, and newspaper reproduction do not apply to posters and photo-murals. They are an excellent way to get photographs out into the street, for instance, so that more people have the opportunity of seeing your work.

Communicating with the public is always a problem though. As the great Expressionist painter Oscar Kokoschka rather cynically put it: 'I and my public understand each other very well: they don't hear what I say, and I don't say what they'd like to hear.'

Photographers rarely take advantage of the scale and position that poster-hoardings afford. But the Side Gallery in Newcastle-upon-Tyne successfully used a photo-mural of an image by Peter Turner to advertise a photographic exhibition held at their gallery in 1977 (Side Gallery, Newcastle-upon-Tyne)

ANNA AND I IN TORQUAY

JUDY AND MYSELF

UNCLE BILL WITH ANNA AND JUDY

DADDY WITH JUDY AND I AT BLACKPOOL

JUDY, ANNA AND MYSELF

The family album is a continuing testimony to the snapshot's position as a great, but unpretentious, folk art. But underlying the apparent innocence and naïvety of the genre, clues can be found concerning human relationships and social history that – if seriously investigated – could be very illuminating and informative

5

THE PHOTOGRAPHER AS WITNESS

The vast majority of photographs are taken in order to make an image that appears to give an accurate representation of the thing photographed.

When you photograph your sister in front of the Eiffel Tower you want your sister to be identified as herself, and the same goes for the Eiffel Tower. You would also like the photograph to confirm that you went to Paris accompanied by your sister,

The largest number of photographs produced are those taken with the aim of both providing ourselves with a souvenir of our travels, and providing other people with evidence that we did actually go there and see and experience those things we said we did. The photograph becomes the evidence, and probably carries more weight than our words (Paul Hill)

and you both visited the Eiffel Tower. Although photographs can be interpreted in many different ways, it would be obvious that a small print of this image in a photographic album would confirm that your intention was to provide yourself with a souvenir of France. This would also unequivocally prove that you had seen the Eiffel Tower. The photograph therefore becomes evidence.

Legal evidence

Photographic evidence in a court of law has as much, perhaps more, validity than verbal testimony. Photographs that show, for example, the position and extent of wounds, or the relationship in a street of a stop-sign and a crashed car, could conclusively prove someone innocent or guilty. The photograph seems honest and incorruptible because it is made by a machine, and apparently, not by man. The camera's apparent objectivity, and the photograph's ability to describe and identify, are among the medium's most valuable attributes. Photographs are also permanent preservable pieces of visual evidence (in a convenient two-dimensional form) that confirm the physical existence of people, objects, places and events.

Snapshots

The snapshot is, of course, the most familiar sort of photography. With the 'idiot-proof' design of modern instant cameras anyone can successfully make a photograph. Although you may be influenced by other photographs you see, either in family albums, stores, or publications, the major concern when you start taking pictures is to get the subject in the middle of the viewfinder, whether it is grandfather standing rigidly to attention, or the family's pet dog running round the garden.

The snapshot never comes out as you think it will; it is either better, or worse. As you become more knowledgeable, and photographically sophisticated, there is less uncertainty and, as a result, some of the magic goes. It is impossible to recapture those naïve days and naïvety is one of the major ingredients of snapshots. They are pieces of unpretentious folk art that the professional cannot make. There is great pleasure and fulfilment to be found in making unaffected souvenirs.

Historians and anthropologists can learn a great deal from family snapshot albums and we can as well. It is fascinating to see how our great-grandparents looked and dressed; it is pleasurable to relive through our 'snaps' those summer adventures when we were children; it is intriguing to work out how people and places have changed through the years. But those dusty pages may do more than jog your memory. Why are some members of your family rarely photographed? Why do some close relatives never stand by each other? What is that little girl who poses with so much assurance doing now? Your investigations and detective work could help build up an interesting family history. It is no coincidence that sociologists and psychologists are beginning to find snapshot albums an invaluable source of revealing information for their researches and analyses. Albums do, of course, distort by omission, as we prefer to record happy, pleasant times, and never think of photographing sad events. It would be thought obscene to 'snap' a funeral, for instance – but why not?

Portraits

Photographs, of whatever type, are made by people for people, so it is understandable that the most common subject matter in photography should be human beings. The feature that identifies a person most conclusively is the face. Our physiognomy may not be as unique as our fingerprints, but it usually distinguishes us clearly from each other.

A picture of a face is called a *portrait*, but is a photograph of facial features a true portrait? Does a picture of your eyes, ears, nose, mouth and hair really depict you accurately: Alfred Stieglitz once said that a true portrait should be a series of photographs of a person taken at regular intervals 'between the cradle and the grave'.

When we make contact with each other we do so with our eyes. If anonymity is thought desirable, the eyes are covered; on a photograph by a black line (e.g. photographs of prisoners in newspapers) or, in reality, by wearing dark glasses or a mask. It seems that if you cannot make eye-to-eye contact with people in a photograph you cannot really identify them. But anonymity is usually the last thing that most people want in portraiture. We want to be able to recognise the individual who has been photographed.

A photographic portrait is therefore often used by two very different sections of society – the police and the publicity business. Your face can be your fortune if you are an actor, but it can be quite the opposite if you are a criminal!

Portraiture was the first major commercial application of photography in the 19th century and it was not long before almost every town in the world had a portrait photographer. Despite the phenomenal growth of amateur portrait photography, there is still a great demand for professional portrait photographs, whether they end up in a passport or in a boardroom. It may be vanity that motivates people to have images of them-

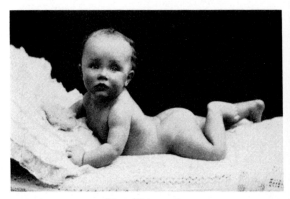

Me at 8½ months

Me at 44 years 9 months

These pictures of photographer Jo Spence have a strong chronological relationship. Combined with other portraits taken through the years – reflecting changing physical and emotional states – a reasonably true picture of her life emerges (Jo Spence/Photography Workshop)

selves recorded, or perhaps it is an attempt to achieve some kind of immortality.

The professional attempts to capture the personality of his subject by use of light, angle of view and, above all, by 'freezing' a revealing expression that reflects the individual's character. But the way a photograph is taken may often say more about the photographer's style than about the person being photographed. The photographer may give an accurate impression of his subject but the result could, on the other hand, be unintentionally defamatory. Like a hunter, the photographer frequently wants to 'capture' an expression or gesture. This can be done in a *confrontive*, or a *candid* way. The portrait 'victim' can either be very conscious of the photographer or totally unaware of his presence. Consequently, the results will be as different as the approaches.

A *posed portrait* can be just as revealing as a picture of a person 'taken on the wing', although the latter will appear more candid and natural. The former approach shows how people react to the camera; how they position themselves; what they wear and so on. If you let your subjects choose where and how they wish to be photographed, the pictures may disclose more about them despite the apparent artificiality of the situation. You also have a closer, more direct, relationship with the person which leads to a more responsible attitude towards them as a subject,

Facial identity distinguishes us from each other, and the major feature for individual recognition is the eyes. When they are covered – as in this photograph taken in a women's prison – the individual cannot be recognised, and it is therefore 'safe' to publish the photograph

rather than a 'victim'. If you prefer to conceal yourself from the subject you may obtain a satisfactory 'slice-of-life' but is it a more truthful portrayal of a person than the posed picture?

Many people hate being photographed because it makes them feel self-conscious. In other words, it forces them to become acutely aware of their own appearance at both the time of posing and later when they see their photographic image.

It may sound like a contradiction in terms but it may not always be necessary for people to actually appear in portraits. A detailed photograph of the interior of a room may portray the personality of the occupants more accurately than any picture of their head and shoulders. After all, we usually gather around us the things we like or are interested in. A photograph of these items could be more *you* than a photograph of your face.

When eye-to-eye contact is lost (as in these two photographs) people become anonymous (Jamie Parslow, Deborah Baker)

Because our face is the front we present to the world, it may inevitably be a mask too. When the camera freezes an expression the mask-like impression can be reinforced. Politicians are continuously in the public's eye, and probably feel they have to appear serious people. However, there is usually more than one side to everyone, as these two photographs of Enoch Powell, MP, show (Paul Hill)

A posed portrait can be very revealing, particularly if the positioning is up to the sitter. This leader of a local branch of the extreme right-wing National Front organisation chose to be photographed in front of the Front emblem. He also selected the position and the expression that he would adopt for the camera. The man appears not only to be confronting the camera, but also the people who will eventually see the photograph (Paul Hill)

The *environmental portrait* is one of the most convincing and informative forms of portraiture, as it attempts to relate the subject to his or her working or home background. This type of portrait may be posed or candid, but it is only successful if the link between the subject and the environment is appreciated by the viewer.

For example, a man in a room full of paintings could be an artist, a museum curator, or an electrician just about to mend the lights. If you want to convey the fact that the man is an artist there are two methods you can adopt. You either control the shooting by posing the man in front of the paintings with a palette and brushes in his hand, or you wait until the man makes a characteristic action, such as painting, and shoot then. The latter approach demands patience, perception, and quick reflexes. The man may only be painting for a very brief time and you may be badly positioned so that the background is inappropriate, and, therefore, if photographed, the juxtaposition may well confuse the viewer. Quick footwork, a change of angle, and you may have got a successful environmental portrait, especially if the lighting, focusing, depth of field and shutter speed are correct. But with this approach the most important thing is to capture the moment which combines the right information, gesture and composition. In other words, both content *and* form should be incorporated for the picture to be successful.

[*Content* means the presentation of the subject matter in a picture – the 'facts' of the subject are represented in such a way that they are recognisable and understandable in a specific context. *Form*, in photography, refers to the arrangement or 'gestures' of shapes made by the tones, not necessarily by the objects photographed.]

The disclosive nature of a posed portrait – as far as the subject is concerned – may be suspect and, in fact, say more about the photographer than the 'victim'. When you photograph people whose way of life and standards are different to your own, the responsibility to the 'victims' is greater. The need to be 'fair' to them and yourself is emphasised in these situations. Although the photographer may live in a different culture to the gypsy woman he may detect and wish to convey qualities he thinks she exhibits that are universal (Paul Hill)

Even photographs of people we may be more familiar with, like the middle-class couple here, can seem like an anthropological study
(John Myers)

The interior of a room empty of people can be a wonderful subject for exploring formal photographic relationships in a controlled situation, but it can also provide a convincing portrait of the owner. In this photograph certain clues, as to the identity of the inhabitant, are detectable. The pictures on the wall and mirror look like those that a girl would have in her room. The plastic necklace and the marionette indicate that the girl is a sub-teenager, though the bicycle lamp could mean she is older. But it is probably used by the family as a hand torch. The dressing table looks as if it were bought from a cheap antique shop, or auction, by the parents, who could easily be young and middle class (Mary Cooper)

The documentary approach to portraiture usually places the subject in an identifiable environment. In this case the subject is an Asian who works in an English iron foundry. The picture not only conveys his working conditions, but also highlights his isolation, even during rest periods (Paul Hill)

Documentary photographs

It may be wrong to claim that photographs never lie, but photographs can be used together with other information, to show the facts of a situation and lead to a 'truthful' assessment of it. Photographers committed to the *in-depth documentary* approach do not look for the single picture that attempts to 'tell the story'. Their aim is to piece together visual evidence in order to construct an honest document which communicates the reality of a situation as the photographer (or team of photographers) sees it. This sort of work can never be totally objective but if the document reflects thorough knowledge and involvement, it at least indicates a point of view which has been acquired from long-term personal experience. There are

many sociological and political applications of this type of photography; social conditions are most frequently the subject matter for the committed documentarian.

The documentarian's finished work is usually seen in an exhibition, a book, or a pamphlet, often with accompanying written text or tape recordings. The text and tapes may contain the actual words of people photographed, or other participants connected with the photographer's project. These are used to complement the photographs and to ensure that the audience is given every opportunity to understand what is going on in the pictures. The true documentarian does not aim for an esoteric product which only a few people can

In-depth documentary photography attempts to 'get under the skin' of a place, an event, or a social problem. The photographer has to spend a long time piecing together visual (and sometimes oral) evidence in order to get something approaching a true document that fairly represents the subject matter. Nick Hedges spent two years, with the help of a photographic fellowship, photographing in five Midland factories. He wanted to show the working people whom he believes are responsible for producing the wealth upon which our society depends. He interviewed many of the workers and extracts from these interviews accompanied the exhibition, which was the culmination of the project (see also pages 69, 70)

understand. Communication with, and comprehension by, a mass audience should be the aim with this type of photography.

One of the best ways to reach a mass audience is via newspapers, but they tend to deal with single pictures and may not be interested in most documentary work unless there is a topical, 'newsy' peg on which to hang the photograph(s). The largest mass audience is the television viewing public and that is why many documentary photographers move into film. They also tend to stay there.

News magazines often have a large international readership. As well as stories illustrated by single pictures, they publish picture stories and photo-essays. *Picture stories* usually revolve round an important news event like a war, a state visit, a major weather disaster, and so on. A team of photographers is dispatched to the location and they cover as many aspects of the story as they are able to. All the photographs are sent back as soon as possible and the ones to be published are selected by a small team of editors and designers. *One* photographer may obtain the best pictures (he or she may have been in the 'prime' position) but it is essentially a team effort.

A *photo-essay*, on the other hand, is generally done by one person and is not usually about a news item. Narrative is important and normally each essay should have a beginning, middle and end, as those kind of stories – in literature *and* photography – are always the easiest to understand and to enjoy. This form of visual communication has no language barriers and should

(a)

(b)

The pictures in a photo-essay have to combine together to form a story-line that is comprehensible to the reader. In this photo-essay on the annual horse fair at Appleby in the north of England, the narrative is as follows: People arrive at the fair (a) – giving the reader an idea of the location; the horses are washed (b), rinsed (c), and dried out (d), before being tied up for the potential buyers to examine (e); then the sale is confirmed with a slap of the hands (f), before a relaxing and celebratory drink (g), followed by an afternoon nap (h). This seems a very simplistic scenario, which has no central theme or character, but, nonetheless, assumes there is one. But the photographer is not being dishonest by stringing the pictures together in this way, as all these things do happen at this particular event. Photography can after all only suggest the narrative, captions do the rest (Paul Hill)

(c)

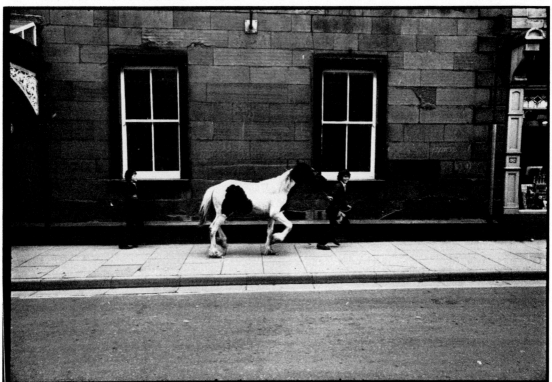

(d)

(e)

(f)

(g)

(h)

When major news events occur, magazines and newspapers dispatch small teams of photographers to cover them. Sometimes a photographer captures the action surrounding the event in a very dramatic way, as in this picture by Bryn Campbell of anti-Nazi rioters being sprayed by a water cannon in Germany

therefore be universally comprehensible. This makes the photo-essay a classic mode for poetically transmitting information. The overall structure of the photo-essay is very important. The images (like those conjured up in poems) made around one part of the story must be linked with those made around the next and carried through the whole essay. You obviously have to concentrate on one part of the story at a time, but you should never lose sight of the narrative concept of the project.

There are some basic points worth remembering when considering the making of a photo-essay. An 'establishing' picture of the location gives the reader a general view of the physical area involved. If people are included – and they usually are in photo-essays – try and show the rela-

tionships between them. If there is a central character attempt to give him or her an identity that the viewer can comprehend. You know your subject's occupation, but the reader does not, unless you are able to visually transmit the fact through your pictures. Similarly, when photographing an event – it, too, should be given an identity. The action at the event will often be self-explanatory if it is a familiar or common occurrence, but if it is outside the reader's personal knowledge or culture then it may be baffling. A photo-essay of such a situation should attempt to explain what is happening. Remember that the reader is not there with you.

Momentous national and international events can be even harder to narrate visually. How can a photographer adequately show, in a series of

The scale of a war can be extremely difficult to convey in photographs, but the tragedy of it can always be seen in the faces of the innocent victims. The true cost of war is shown in this picture by Don McCullin of a woman who has just lost her husband in the fighting on the island of Cyprus in 1964

pictures, let alone a single image, the scale of a war or the enormity of a disaster? All that you can probably do is to indicate the *cost* in human suffering. This can often be seen most vividly in the expressions on people's faces. It can also be hinted at through telling, or even ironic juxtapositioning of incongruous or contrasting subjects. Action pictures on their own rarely convey the horror of war as most military conflicts are conducted at long distance and it is impossible (or suicidal) to approach closely. Still photographs cannot convey what it feels like to experience an earthquake or a flood. All they can do is to show isolated fragments from the continuing action; but, like jigsaw pieces, together they may form a reasonably true and comprehensible 'picture' of the event. The individual *parts* may make up a significant *whole*. The human mind may be able to make sense of the many facets of great events and understand their implications, but all the photographer can do is attempt to distil what is happening in front of the camera for the reader.

The photographer *has* to be where the action is, and only the photographs taken there can count. Photographs cannot give objective overviews; that is the function of the theoretician, not the photographer. The way the images are read may be fundamentally different to the photographer's intentions. Captions can be used to help direct the reader, but their response can never be accurately anticipated. However, there are many instances where public opinion and social change have been affected by photographers' pictures. This can be extremely gratifying, particularly when deprivation and injustices are remedied, but history has shown us that photographic propaganda can be a double-edged sword.

The interpretation of photographs can be very problematic despite the photographer's attempts to direct the reader toward.
1977 was a tricky situation to photograph as militants frequently attempt to make media capital out of such incidents. The media
Steele-Perkins show two different sides of the riot. In one, a demonstrator appears to be a 'victim' of police action, and in the second
magazine, caption writers could influence your reading of them by what they wrote under the pictures. Frequently

standing of the situation as he/she saw it. The violent clash between National Front marchers and anti-racists in Lewisham, London in
*pret this riot in conflicting ways. They tended to use the photographs that supported their view of the clash. These two pictures by Chris
*n' is a policeman. Everyone interprets these images according to their own political feelings, but it is easy to see how newspaper, or
icture would be published, so the photographer's attempt to give a 'fair' coverage of the clash would be negated

"DOVEDALE CHURCH ROCK, DOVEDALE.   4479   G.W.W.

This kind of 'scene' from Dovedale was typical of the sort recorded by writers of guidebooks in the mid-19th century. They were responding to the new and burgeoning industry of tourism. Photographers like George Washington Wilson were not slow to climb on that bandwagon by providing local shops and hotels with this kind of photograph to sell to visitors. By the 1880s – when this picture was taken – Wilson's firm was the biggest producer of topographical views in Britain, turning out at least 10,000 photographic prints a week (Author's Collection)

6

TRAVELS WITH A CAMERA

When you visit somewhere, what are the things you photograph to remember that place by? Why does everyone seem to select the same scenes — mountains towering over the village in the fore-ground, the evening sun setting over the sea? Is what you photograph affected by the views you see on postcards? It is not surprising that you should be influenced by postcards because there are so many of them around. In the 19th century photographers were equally influenced by the

guidebooks that travellers used then. When photo-graphers visited a picturesque site, they used the current guidebook and positioned themselves to get the same view in the photograph that was so eloquently described in the book.

At the time there was a 'wonders-of-nature' love affair between 19th century aesthetes and the landscape. The celebration of Nature, manifested through painting and photography, was partly a form of immunisation against the seemingly soul-

This gloriously romantic view by Francis Bedford (c. 1870) was typical of the type of photograph you could buy at the time from the local post office, or village shop, near to the spot where it was taken. As the Victorian photographers were influenced by the romantic landscape painters of their day, so generations of photographers have followed the pictorial landscape style which emerged at that time. The silky-smooth surface of the stream is caused by the long exposure it was then necessary to give to get a printable negative
(Author's Collection)

less march of industrialisation. Ironically, the technological advances that industrialisation heralded later also led to the development of roll-film and smaller, less complicated cameras which made photography available to the masses. It was no longer solely the pursuit of well-heeled gentlefolk, or commercial high-street operators.

Landscape and nature

How do you feel when you experience nature? How do you feel when you stand on a high point and gaze at the landscape in front of you? Is what you photograph what you feel? Can your reactions be conveyed in a photograph anyway? A photograph which attempts to show simply how wonderful nature is poses very few visual questions. It is a conservative artefact because it celebrates the status quo. The photographer, it appears, can only state: 'Isn't this a magnificent view. It must be preserved. It should never be spoiled.'

The use of photography to promote conservation was particularly evident in the USA in the late 1800s. Photographs of remote and wild areas persuaded the authorities to establish certain parts of the USA (e.g. Yellowstone) as national parks, preserved for posterity in all their natural, untouched splendour.

Magnificent photographs of the landscape, like this mountain view by Bradford Washburn taken in 1960 are very striking. The sensuous undulations of the pure white snow catch your attention first, but when you notice the tiny figures of the mountaineers and their line of footprints, you become aware of the scale. You are able to relate – but from a comfortable vantage-point – to the human activity taking place (Museum of Science, Boston)

Why do we hold the *natural landscape* in so much awe? Is it because we feel so small in it and, therefore, a little fearful? Landscape *photographs* are comfortable and reassuring by comparison. Of course, if we were actually at the place photographed our sensory faculties would respond completely differently to the way they react when viewing the photograph. A photograph of a landscape can be warm and appealing – so different to actually being there and having to cope with the physical exertion, the weather, and so on.

What moves us to call something like a sunset '*beautiful*'? As we cannot make actual contact with such an ephemereal thing as a sunset, we must, therefore, be moved, when we refer to it as 'beautiful', by *our* admiration and appreciation of

it. Objects do not have '*beauty*' in the sense of possessing a thing called 'beauty'. We impose the word 'beauty' on things and what makes it confusing is that there is no water-tight consensus on what 'beauty' actually is. Maybe we feel a sense of harmony, a soothing sensation, or a 'gut' feeling, when we contemplate, what are for us 'beautiful' things. Beauty is a thing you have to feel inwardly – never assume that what you think of as beautiful is going to be appreciated as beautiful by anybody else. And never let people brainwash you into accepting that their definition of beauty is the only valid one.

'Beautiful' is also a convenient word frequently used to describe pictures, but it is an imprecise one, like 'nice'. It is much easier to appreciate the

There is a great attraction to this popular photograph of Heptonstall, Yorkshire by Fay Godwin, because it is 'beautiful' by our cultural standards. There may be a feeling of the unknown and mysterious, especially in a religious context (note the position of the church), but there is a warm feeling of harmony and timelessness in the picture too. It is not so much about spiritual illumination, as about idyllic escapism

way someone crafts something, or the manner in which a photographer presents his/her work, or the explanation the maker gives concerning his/her photographs.

But do 'beautiful' photographs – to return to the conservation issue – nonetheless persuade thousands of people to go to certain attractive and wild areas, thereby endangering their unspoilt character? The compulsion to find out how reality compares with a photograph is very powerful.

Photographs that promote the *picturesque* may be pleasant and soothing but they confirm an idea of pastoral bliss which may not be quite accurate. Is there a cement factory or an open-cast mine lurking just out of frame beyond the leafy bower

and the twinkling stream? And if there are such things there, is it not more honest to include them in the picture too? Will not the juxtapositioning of the 'ugly' and the 'beautiful' make the viewer more aware of what mankind is doing to the natural landscape?

But even 'ugly' man-made things can be beautiful if they are photographed with aesthetics in mind. Grim factory walls may 'imprison' exploited workers and dirty mines may 'scar' the countryside, but that does not mean that photographers have avoided making beautiful photographs of such things. Beauty is in the eye of the beholder, but to the camera's 'neutral' eye all subjects are seen in the same way. Light is the

The 'beauty' of a river estuary, and the 'ugliness' of a dockland area, are juxtaposed by Ron McCormick in this picture taken in Newport, South Wales. But maybe the things convention tells us are 'ugly' in actuality are 'beautiful' in a photographic print. Industrial scars and environmental pollution can make 'beautiful' photographs

Buildings can be photographed in a very straightforward way, or in a manner that evokes a mood or atmosphere. Lewis Baltz's photograph of a housing development in Park City, USA, is a presentation of a building site in accurate photographic detail, whereas Graham Smith's picture from Newcastle-upon-Tyne conveys a mood by his interpretation of the light falling on the building and the street

same whether it is reflected off terracotta tiles or corrugated iron. Photographs of walls on their own will never show imprisonment, but, ironically, barbed wire round a nature reserve might. But you should not let such paradoxes confound you – better to exploit them!·

Man-made landscape

The topography of a place may also, of course, show the obvious influence of man. Many photographers prefer this form of landscape to the one created by nature. There is a fascination in what civilisation constructs and leaves behind. Much visual pleasure and cultural and historical information can be gained from photographing

what man has built. Buildings can be photographed in order to show their grandeur or their monumentality, the skill of the architect or the builder, or to evoke mood and atmosphere.

The *straight approach* is the best one if the photographer wishes to be objective. With this approach the aim is to allow the subject to speak for itself. To photograph *the thing itself* means just that. The presentation of the object(s) in accurate photographic detail, is sufficient; its qualities should be self-evident, and interpretation by the photographer unnecessary. The aim is to intensify the viewer's awareness of the subject matter. Large format view-cameras are often used to obtain this visual clarity. (Advertising photographers also use the same technique for their still-life 'pack-shots' to emphasise the fine quality of the product being promoted.)

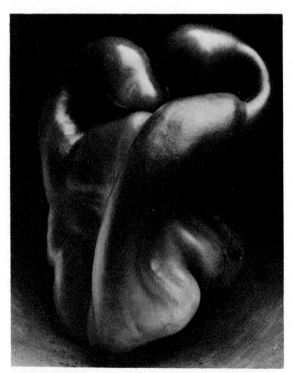 

Natural, and man-made, objects photographed in quintessential detail can celebrate 'the thing itself' by intensifying the viewer's awareness of the subject matter. These two classic studies, one by Edward Weston (Pepper No. 30, 1930), and the other by Paul Strand (Lathe, New York, 1923) are perfect examples of the 'straight' style of photography which directed the medium away from sentimentally romantic pictorialism towards a more photographically objective approach. The consummate craftmanship employed in the making of these prints also displayed the inherent qualities of the 'fine' print (courtesy of the Estate of Edward Weston; courtesy of the Estate of Paul Strand)

The image of the dark satanic mills of northern England – all dirt and deprivation – appears to be portrayed in this photograph of Halifax taken by Bill Brandt in the 1930s. But the stylised manner of printing make it an excellent example of chiaroscuro, *rather than social documentation. The documentary photograph becomes an art object*

The propensity for photography to 'beautify' everything can clearly be seen in these two exquisite photographs – one of a factory, and the other of an office block. These normally 'unbeautiful' subjects are transformed in one case into a graphic and tonal exercise, and in the other a visual poem about light and scale (Lewis Baltz, Michael Ormerod)

The home environment

When we think of places to photograph we rarely consider our own immediate environment; probably because we cannot see any interest in what is nearest to us. We feel that the interesting and the unusual lie far away – 'the grass is always greener on the other side'. But the search for *exotica* can often be anti-climactic, and the only pictures produced are conventional views which confirm that you went to an interesting place whilst the rest of us stayed at home. Photographs have to generate more than envy in the viewer. They should attempt to illuminate and excite, not reinforce a stereotyped vision of the world that we are often in danger of receiving from teachers, commerce, or from the media. It is necessary to try to capture the mood and spirit of a place (whether it be 5,000 miles or 50 yards away from where we live) if you want to reveal anything original. There could be as much grandeur in a photograph of forms made by the light and shade on the back wall of your house as there is in the shot of a distant mountain range.

With the easy availability of jet travel and relatively cheap package tours exotica are easily reached, and as we are all aware photographs are used to help sell the 'magic-carpet' dream. Consequently, we always get a favourable image of places from holiday brochures. The idealised visions they peddle rarely correspond with reality because tour operators believe the customer wants 'paradise' rather than truth.

The search for the exotic does not have to take you to faraway places. Night shots in leafy, mock-Tudor suburbia can reveal some strange things too. So it may be a good idea to look in your own backyard before embarking on journeys to unusual places and foreign lands. Horse-chestnut leaves can look like tropical plants when their shadows are cast by light, in this case from an ordinary street lamp (Paul Hill)

The 'fine' print

The idea of *beauty* may be central to the way you photograph a landscape, whether it is formed by nature, or by man. This beauty should be echoed in the photographic print – when the quality of vision and the excellence of craft come together. If you feel an affinity with the landscape, this can be brought out in the warmth of the tones in the print. In bromide and chloro-bromide printing papers, brown/olive-green tones gives this type of warmth, whereas blue/black tones have a comparative coldness. If the landscape is bleak and harsh, the latter tonal quality should be used. The tonal 'colour' can also be altered by using different print developers.

The type of surface of the paper is also important. A *matt* surface will appear 'dead' in comparison to a *glossy* surface, because it is a poor reflector of light. But too much gloss (or a glazed finish) gives a mirror effect which can make the tonal separation difficult to see because of the high reflection of light off the surface. An unglazed glossy surface is an excellent compromise. Paper emulsions which contain more silver give more detail and richness in the darker tones. The way the paper is coated with the various necessary chemical compositions can also radically effect its 'luminosity'. Many photographers prefer a porcelain-like surface as this has a sensuality which may correspond to the surface of the objects photographed. Some photographers coat their own papers so they can obtain the tone and surface texture they require. But be careful of too much fetishism in printing, as a luscious print can often mask a thin idea.

7

IN SEARCH OF SELF AND THE METAPHOR

Photographs that set out to be metaphors for the feelings of the photographer are difficult to accomplish and are rarely easy to understand straightaway. To attempt to show our emotions, state of mind, or psyche in photographs could appear futile, given the 'objectivity' of the medium. Emotions can be difficult to portray because of their ephemeral quality; but as they govern much of our behaviour and continuously affect our lives, they can hardly be ignored.

To photograph what you feel rather than what is in front of the camera can seem a daunting task given the medium's representational facility. The metaphor can also appear inscrutable if too much emphasis is laid on deciphering the objects in the picture. The wooden stakes impaling the anonymous body of a person (who appears to be about to be guillotined), whilst strange animals in human clothing lurk amongst the trees can be recognised and mentally catalogued. But on an emotional level, what does the image evoke in the viewer? (Opposite) By including his shadow, the photographer has inevitably personalised the image. The ambiguity in the picture is used to increase the sense of unease that can often come from ordinary situations photographed in a very subjective way. The swimming pool rails become his 'arms', the water appears to be a featureless abyss, and the concrete in the foreground looks like the sky (Paul Hill)

The psychological approach does, of course, make the photographer very vulnerable, as the pictures may be embarrassingly personal, or overbearingly symbolic, but if your emotions and inner feelings are honestly expressed then you will be less likely to be accused of pretentiousness.

Self-expression

Even if photographers produce highly subjective 'psychological' photographs, the influences of their particular culture and society are bound to be expressed. One's *self* is a fundamental part of subjective thinking, and thus of conveying feeling within a photograph. As a member of a society you should try and reflect the feelings of others as

well as your own, because 'you' are an integral part of 'them'.

As a photographer you record what is 'out there in the world' and so you have to select from all that wealth of material the specific motifs which can act as vehicles for your inner feelings. The selection you make reveals how you feel – or want to appear to feel – about the subject: its content or its form. In that sense all photographs, are to some extent, *self-portraits* whether you directly include yourself in the picture or not. You can, of course, incorporate yourself in the image obliquely by showing your shadow or reflection – although these used to be considered photographic faults. Alternatively you may use another person or object to represent your *alter ego*.

The appearance of the photographer in the actual image should not be considered egocentric. It may simply show that the photographer wants to put himself or herself 'on the line', in preference

The inclusion of one's self *in the photograph, physically and/or metaphorically, can seem embarrassing, but it is usually the most revelatory thing that you can do with the camera. Sexual and gender roles and performances are hinted at in this photograph. A woman photographer photographs herself in a seemingly clumsy way that denies the possibility of a stereotyped 'aware' pose. This increases her vulnerability by removing the opportunity for her to know what the camera is doing (Angela Kelly)*

The photographers' shadow in a photograph used to be thought of as a mistake, but it can be a most effective device to indicate your direct involvement in the image you are making. You can also indulge in a sense of play by distorting your shadow to make it seem more threatening (Paul Hill)

to 'hiding' behind the people, places, and events in front of the camera.

Some hint of your personality always emerges from your photographs even if they were just meant to be records. Other people can often perceive the 'real' you coming out in your pictures – the trick is to try to divine the personally significant images for yourself. If you succeed in finding this out, you are better equipped when it comes to making the sort of photographs that are most relevant – and revelatory – to others.

Reflecting the human condition

You may find that you often photograph your *family* – the institution that probably affects you the most (positively and negatively!). If you care deeply about those nearest and dearest to you, it

will be noticeable in the pictures. Anyway, why photograph subjects you may feel ambivalent about when those you really care for reside in the same house as you? The ordinary and the extraordinary things connected with existence – the joys and the traumas – often happen in and around your home and family. This should be reflected in your photographs of them.

Human beings are very curious (in both senses of the word) animals and our attention is frequently attracted by the strange behaviour of others. Photographers continually photograph the behaviour and actions of their fellow humans; they even diligently search them out. But must the photographer always be the hunter? Is he not a victim too? Photographers are part of society and just as vulnerable to its vagaries as anyone else. By metaphorically holding up a mirror to ourselves we may symbolise more than our own vulnerability – we could echo some of the emotions and

Emmet Gowin has used his family as a continuing motif for his photography. In the first photograph, a moment is caught when nearly all the family seem lost in their own thoughts. The family resemblances are revealed in this tableau, but so is each person's individuality. The water-melon pieces are devices which give the image an initial focal point for the eye to radiate from

Quiet, apparently 'secret', places found by the more introspective photographers seem imbued with a mystery, or some inexplicable quality, that they find attractive. They attempt to transmit that quality through the print, so that it can be contemplated in the same way as the natural scene (John Blakemore)

an act of faith. It would be invidious to attribute any objective significance to the subject matter in such photographs. The aim is to appreciate their symbolic and metaphoric qualities – the picture should transcend the physical nature of things.

Often these photographers seek locations which evoke a certain atmosphere or *'spirit of place'*. They wish their images to transmit an ethereal 'presence' (despite the seemingly mechanistic and utilitarian nature of photography). They hope their photographs will be imbued with an 'otherness' that is reality to them. This approach has a spiritual quality that verges on mysticism and thus alienates a great many people, who prefer a more rational use of photography. These photographers also have a tendency to make fine quality prints which then become precious objects in their own right: not out of pretentiousness, but because it is also a part of the experience for the print to be a 'fine' thing too. The print is an object to be cared about in a world where most photographs are not. It is an artefact to be contemplated and meditated upon.

The natural landscape is nearly always the motif used for this kind of work. But a 'spirit of place' can be felt in some man-made locations such as the interior of a building, for instance, as well as in the deepest woodland.

What is important is the *intuitive* response to a situation. There is often an instinctive appeal of a place which is difficult to pinpoint but is nonetheless, there: like some unseen force of attraction. Of

97

(a)

(b)

(c)

In a personal 'sequence', the visual and/or emotional interrelation and correlation of images should be aimed for, rather than a chronological, or purely intellectual, progression. In (a) and (b) the gesture of the hands and their contact with opaque surfaces provide a link. The shape of the telephone poles in (b) is echoed by the road and the rock ledge in (c), where, again, a part of the body is used metaphorically. The arrow-like triangular shape – evident in (a), (b) and (c) – surrounds the head in (d). The ledge of (c) and the edge of the swimming pool in (d) are horizontal objects that have become vertical with the edge in (d) seeming to push the head (and, therefore, the focal point) out of the picture. The human figure becomes more dominating again in (e) – perhaps it is the person in (d)? The wedge shape appears again – this time surrounding a cricket match. The central motif of this 'sequence' is children, whose innocent activities have been transformed by the photographer into apparently stressful situations. In the same way as children overdramatise their play, so the photographer has used the camera to dramatically draw attention to the tension and anxiety that pervades many people's lives every day; not only in visual terms, but by using the most vulnerable beings in our society as the thread that holds the 'sequence' together (Paul Hill)

(d)

(e)

Photographs are used by many photographers as 'equivalents' to inner feelings that are about the spiritual as well as the psychological. One of the finest exponents of this approach was Minor White whose picture of the Grand Tetons, USA, attempts to transcend the physicality of what is in front of the camera in order to produce something he sees as almost sacred (courtesy of Minor White Archive, Princeton University)

course, the intellect, rather than the instinct, plays a major role when it comes to *how* the photographs are made. But the emotional and sensory reaction to something is often a stronger motivator than the intellectual one.

More 'sense' can be made of the picture at the printing stage, as post-visualisation frequently reveals hitherto unknown elements in an image. This can provide an additional 'journey of discovery', but do not expect it to be always a fruitful one. A 'presence' which could be conveyed, for example, through something as transient as light, has to be captured by a camera, just like the fleeting gesture made by someone in the street.

An intimate relationship with the print is crucial in this area of photography and, therefore, the *portfolio* is the best context for such work. Another vital factor is the sequencing of the prints. This is done best by laying out the prints in the order prescribed by the maker and experiencing the interrelation and correlation that takes place. The work should be considered at length before it can 'speak', because at first glance only the 'surface' may be visible. A *sequence* should provide us with an experience that affects us emotionally or spiritually, even subconsciously. It is a psychological document that should be as culturally relevant as any good social document.

This apparently mystical – even ritualistic – approach to photography confounds many people, though they would probably be the first to admit that even in the real world there is still a

The symbolic touching of heads as an 'equivalent' of some human gesture is a posible interpretation of this image, whereas another might be to see the white shape in the centre as the image of a jewel. Photographs are catalysts for the viewers' feelings as well as for the photographers. Many photographers prefer to celebrate the world of the imagination rather than material existence in their work
(Paul Caponigro)

great deal that is mysterious. The interpretation of a photograph can be as varied as the individuals who look at it. If the viewer is unable to appreciate the transcendent aspect of a photograph, at least he or she still has a representation of an object or scene and a finely crafted artefact to enjoy. There is no medium or discipline that can offer so many positive options.

FILING PERSONAL DOCUMENTS

It has only been during the last 20 years or so that there has been any semblance of a universal acceptance of photography as an important medium for personal expression. That does not mean to say that a great deal of subjective work did not take place before that – far from it! But it is only recently that photography has acquired an increasingly respectable place in galleries, museums and public collections. Not so long ago you would be hard-pressed to find any non-amateur or non-applied photography exhibitions taking place almost anywhere in the world. To collect contemporary photographs, which were not about things like steam engines or 'pop' stars, would have been thought of as slightly insane. There were only a very few magazines which published interesting photographs. This was due largely to the limited ambitions of most photographers and also to the insensitivity of those designers (many are still around) who delight in

(Opposite) The alienation and disaffection is easy to see in modern cities and this picture aimed to portray that. The juxtapositioning of the gilt-framed photograph of a rather apprehensive child against the disfiguring graffiti on the outside of the shop may suggest the same. The truncated portrait and the child's expression also symbolise the pathos of a situation in which spiritual claustrophobia and material survival miserably co-exist (Paul Hill)

losing photographs in lay-outs that resemble mosaics, who put captions and headlines on the actual images, or who spread a picture over the page-fold, destroying its effect. If you succeeded in finding a 'gem', because of bad reproduction, it would probably only have the lustre of an unpolished stone. Word-orientated editors and zealous graphic designers were (and in many cases, still are) more than a match for all but the toughest of photographers; and even the few who fought back could be fired for daring to 'interfere' with matters that did not concern them – like the presentation of *their own* photographs.

There is a 'surreal' quality to this photograph of a solitary figure looking ... where? The human presence in many contemporary photographers' work appears somnambulistic and can often hauntingly evoke the bizarre atmosphere of such situations (Deborah Baker)

There is a pervading anxiety in many urban environments which is reinforced by the stories and films of violence and despair seen in the media. Who does the shadow in this picture belong to? What goes on in the chrome and ceramic tiled room where the photograph is taken? The photographer relies on our fear of the unknown and the mysterious to imbue the image with a threatening atmosphere, hinting at an imminent, possibly inescapable, danger (Paul Hill)

New documentary outlets

Paradoxically, one of the events that has affected this fairly recent awakening has been the advent of television. Although it badly wounded the world of news magazines and photo-journalism, it did force many photographers – faced with a diminishing market for their documentary work – to consider new outlets and new forms for their talents.

Many documentarians naturally gravitated to a much more personal approach which reflected their own feelings, points of view, and concerns – and not those of the papers or magazines that they had worked for. They now sought to subjectively record their impressions of the world around them in their private work, which was often subsidised out of earnings from occasional commercial freelance assignments.

As with the 'fine' print landscape photographers' work, exhibitions, portfolios and monographs, not the mass media, became the outlets for this new *art photography*. The art cognescenti were also 'discovering' photography, so many photo-journalists and studio photographers could now actually sell their work like etchers, lithographers and silk-screen artists – and for similar prices too! Photography also became a respectable subject at universities and colleges, warranting the award of an art degree, so a new employment market opened for photographers. Academia replaced commerce, and many photographers now had the opportunity to escape the materialistic world dictated by fads and deadlines, in favour of the comparative haven of commonrooms and long vacations.

Photography has now become academically and artistically respectable (although many think there is still a long way to go) and, understandably, the *introspective mode* is the most fashionable. The emergent personal documentary approach of recent times is not concerned with warm, affirmative magazine-orientated photo-essays, styled as a 'Day in the life of . . .'. It adopts a more realistic – though often sardonic – view of the environment and the workings of modern society as the photographer, rather than an editor, sees them. Most of these personal documents are more than pictorial representations, they normally have an edge to them as the subject matter is usually man-made and is often the street (and all that goes on in and around it).

Surrealism and photography

The inherent ambiguity of photography can be used to emphasise the alienation and disaffection that many photographers perceive in modern society. Photographs can often hauntingly evoke the strangely unreal quality that is apparent in our surroundings.

The bizarre urban landscapes of the 20th century have a *surreal* quality in them which photographers frequently use as a motif. Human beings often appear in these landscapes almost as sleepwalkers. Chance encounters and unusual juxtapositions are important features. The natural landscape has its 'secrets', but a sense of peace and

A photographer who, like many others, was greatly affected by Surrealism is Ralph Gibson, who published a monograph on that theme, called Somnambulist. The hands which appear to be cut off from any body, seem bent on taking over the eerily empty boat. Gibson's book shows many of the photographer's fantasies, which all seem to have a dream-like quality. The surrealist believes that we are controlled by subconscious, as well as by conscious, reason, and that this less predictable but equally powerful force should be given greater expression

Wide-angle lenses are frequently used to produce exaggeratedly surreal pictures. One photographer who has done this most successfully is Bill Brandt. He used an old police camera with a very small fixed aperture to produce this insect's-eye view of the world. Parts of the body become strange landscapes whose size in the photographs inverts our normal perception of them in real life

security tends to pervade it. But a sense of anxiety resides in the metropolis most of the time. Surrealism and photography conspire most effectively in this environment.

Surrealism as a movement, took shape in the 1920s and photography was very much an integral part of it from the beginning. The Surrealists claim that the subconscious harbours a reality other than – but just as strong as – the one we experience in actuality. The movement emerged at a time when many artists were greatly influenced by Freud's dream analyses, and investigations into the subconscious. Artists felt that the subconscious, rather than conscious reason, should guide their work. A great many Surrealistic paintings are strange and exotic fantasies, whereas the most successful surrealistic photographs show how strange the camera makes our everyday world look. In our dreams, our being and our world become distorted – 'unreal' – because our subconscious has taken over. The photographer can show a disjointed view of the world, but that vision is a believable one because we know he or she must be photographing things that really do exist. The *extraordinary*, or 'unreal', is there amongst the *ordinary*, if we have the perception to see it.

The camera's frame is often used as a cutting edge which can appear to truncate people, and objects. Wide-angled lenses, which optically distort, are used to construct exaggeratedly surreal pictures. Feet can be made to appear as big as doors and ears as large as rocks. In this world of visual hyperbole, situations are not what they seem to be. Ordinary objects can become anthropomorphic, and the human form can become a landscape.

Photography can make human faces into masks and tailor's dummies appear human; mirrors and windows often become doorways into a world behind, and beyond, the surface of the print. Such innuendoes frequently echo subconscious fears: an impression made all the more bizarre by our

Light – the photographers' constant inspiration – can do strange things. The shadow cast by the girl's body here forms a man's head, which appears to dominate her. Photographers constantly stumble over the happy accident, but it is the purpose to which you put that piece of luck that counts in the end (Paul Hill)

108

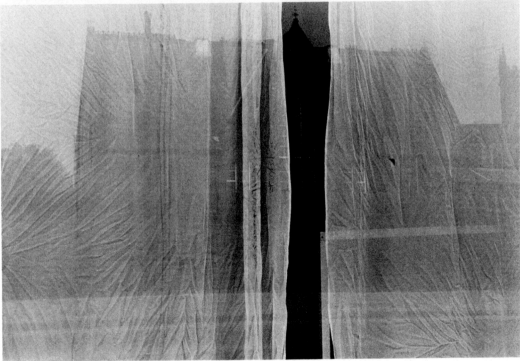

The strange unreality that emanates from photographs of mirrors and windows is a thing that has fascinated Raymond Moore. In the first picture, the dog appears to be framed by a window in the wall. The sunny world, which exists through that window (it is in fact a mirror used to help motorists) is so different from the shadowy one on this side of that implacable wall. The second image appears to be a visual conundrum and merits a long, hard look before you can discover its mystery.

Surreal humour can be found in the most unlikely situations. What is the woman really looking at? How on earth did that telephone kiosk get placed amongst a forest of ferns? Only the photographer knows the answer. But these situations do exist, and their absurdity is accentuated by the camera's ability to abstract. The photographer has to decide though, when the moment, or position, is 'right'
(Paul Hill)

apparently irrational reading of an 'ordinary' object like a photograph.

The uneasy feeling that 'something is about to happen' is often evoked through photographs because the process abstracts and freezes a moment in a continuum that we cannot evade. It takes you out of the *actual* world and places you into the possibly more *real* world of your imagination. The eeriness in photographs of forgotten and forsaken places, for example, is a feeling produced mentally; but what is *physically* there, is a complex of shapes and grey tones. However, the ambiguity of photography makes suggestion into apparent fact and the Surrealist eagerly exploits this. The medium can appear to convey reality and unreality at one and the same time.

Of course, this approach lends itself to overt symbolism and to the obvious metaphoric interpretations of images. But even the most practical of photographers find this area of photography

useful – though most rationalists consider surrealistic photography to be no more than visual *punnery*.

A great deal of surreal humour can be found in the odd and incongruous. Strange juxtapositioning of ordinary objects can be extremely funny, especially if it is achieved naturally. There is nothing deadlier than forced humour.

The modern approach

The plastic and chrome of city centres, the overhead wires and telegraph poles of the asphalt trail, and the shaved lawns and parked cars in suburbia may seem pretty banal subjects, but in recent years this has been the food which has nourished the vision of a great many photographers. The seemingly straight, undramatic, even casual view, however, contains a great deal of often complex

110

Although there seems to be a great deal happening in this picture, there is a lack of 'concrete' information which makes it enigmatic. The air of mystery is heightened by the opening (is it a door, or a window?) onto the sky. Maybe it is a painting of the sky and the building is an art gallery? The photograph alone can never give the answer, but that does not matter. The photograph has become the event (Brian Griffin)

information that at first sight appears mundane, even boring. The images appear to lack strong formal qualities and they are obviously anti-exotic. But the wealth of detail and information bears careful examination and has an exquisite quality that is anything but boring. These minimal *'topographics'* seem bland and featureless – almost clinical. A perfect metaphor for the time out of which they come? Or is this apparently 'dead-pan' recording approach an attempt to move away from *modernist formalism*, in order to make the content of a picture more obvious. It can certainly subvert our usual attachment to the visual 'form' or induced mood of a picture. There is possibly a similar movement in contemporary architecture with the placement of utilities on the outside of buildings. The structure becomes de-fined by the elements that are normally 'covered up' by the architect.

If we agree that photography beautifies most things anyway, we inevitably end up with recognisably *decorative objects*, which may partially explain why people buy photographs to put on their walls, and why photographers are finding more and more patronage, in the form of grants, from arts organisations. If what we call 'art', is being made in the jungle by uncivilised natives *and* by sophisticates in skyscrapers, there must be some fundamental need to do it which transcends the fame-and-fortune ethic. But having said that: a great many people are rather suspicious and cynical about photographers calling themselves artists. Is the democratic potential of the medium stunted by its involvement with the art world?

111

This mundane section of landscape can appear uninteresting – even boring – on first inspection, but the information it contains may merit further examination. The 'extraordinary' usually resides within the 'ordinary' but the search may not be easy. First glance 'impact' can be very transitory. If you want a photograph to last, it may not be a good thing for all its secrets to be revealed too quickly (Paul Hill)

The parked cars and shoe-box houses of suburbia can appear pretty banal subject matter, but not for a photographer like Robert Adams. His approach seems as bland as much of his subject matter, but it is a very precise one. This cool, almost clinical style may be an attempt to move away from overt abstraction and fast-shooting street photography, to a classic mode, reminiscent of the 19th century topographical photographers

The empty landscape – and the minimally detailed photograph of it – has an hypnotic effect. This may be because the eye searches for some recognisable form to rest upon. But like an outwardly featureless lunar landscape, this picture by Harry Callahan positively celebrates its 'nothingness'. You have to let yourself be sucked into it. Minute examination may reveal something to you – or it may not. It all depends on the attitude of mind of the viewer

One of the things that Conceptualists attempted was to eschew what they thought was aesthetic mumbo-jumbo. The fanciful language of 'expressionism' was too imprecise. There is, however, an implied wry comment on the current vogue for language-centred art in this picture of Keith Arnatt.

9

PHOTOGRAPHY, POLITICS AND THE *AVANTE-GARDE*

The cynicism voiced by many people concerning photography's 'elevation' in the art world is symptomatic of the 'anti-art' movement that has become increasingly voluble over the last ten years. Though it must be said that the unease many photographers and critics feel about the Fine Art world has been lurking around for much longer than that. Wherever our loyalties lie we cannot ignore the fact that the continuing debate of the last decade has brought in its wake an increasing amount of extremely valuable analysis and research into the use and history of photography.

Of course, the cynics on the 'art' side of the fence would argue that too much theorising leads to over-verbalisation, and as a consequence virtually negates the use of photography altogether. If every image needs to be dissected and discussed at great length, then why bother to take it in the first place? Do you need a post-mortem to enhance your enjoyment of Beethoven or Gershwin unless you are a musicologist? But one supposes that even the most fervent 'image-analyser' would not wish to stem the flow of contemporary photographic production despite the millions of photographs that already exist in the world to be examined.

The *theoretical* approach to photography seems to have two branches: one that concerns itself with the visual nature and process of the medium and one that seeks to analyse the socio-political relevance in/of photographs. This is an over-simplified breakdown, but it may, at least, be a starting point.

Although both approaches can be categorised as conceptual (i.e. concerned with ideas), the roots are different. However, there is a great deal of cross fertilisation. The first movement comes out of art practice, but is a reaction against art institutions and aestheticism, and the second has emerged from the world of dissident politics, but uses the weapon of polemic instead of the 'objective' documentary mode.

Conceptual photography

The Conceptualists, who sprang from art practice, rebelled against the influence of traditional Art History and the philosophies that said Art was only to do with aesthetics. This parallels the activists in the Dada 'anti-art' movement, which began during the First World War. Many of them work outside the confines of the studio – creating large structures unsuitable for art institutions and conventional tastes, rearranging nature, or conducting performances. These 'events' are often temporary and the only way they become 'fact' is by recording them via the camera. The representation through photography was originally thought to be of secondary importance to the 'act', but more recently the artists have begun to be attracted to the photographic print as the *primary* object.

'Utilitarian' photography is, on the surface, descriptive and unmystical: everyone can recognise what is going on. It is also a new discipline without all the arcane trappings of painting. The photographic approach seems factual rather than intuitive and this lends credence to the theoretical, logical and systematic ethos of the new art. This also ties in with an increasing interest amongst artists in science, new technologies, information theory, semiotics and so on. The camera is a machine with limitations and controls that affect things like exposure and focusing; and is, therefore, a respectable phenomenon to explore. This apparently naïve attitude angers 'old guard' photographers who have been known to sarcastically refer to the Conceptualists' approach as 'let's pretend'. But one must remember that photography *is* new to the products of art academies: those institutions that have fostered amongst their students a dependence on the art market and its dealers who are only interested in 'one-offs' and limited editions. Photography seems an alternative

115

A sculpture left by the tide, Cornwall, 1970

Reflections in the Little Pigeon River, Great Smokey Mountains, Tennessee, 1970

Many artists, like Richard Long, wish to move away from the conventional practice and philosophies of art. He is most interested in natural subjects. The only way that his landscape 'rearrangements' can be experienced by an audience is through photography. His titles may seem rather banal but they are probably deliberately ambiguous, which may lead you to question your perception of what you are really looking at

FACING THE SETTING SUN

A VIEW FROM BREDON HILL OF THE MALVERN HILLS
THE HEREFORDSHIRE BEACON IS ON THE CENTRE HORIZON

SKYLINE RIDGE

A ONE NIGHT WALK BY THE LIGHT OF A FULL MOON

FROM BREDON HILL IN THE VALE OF EVESHAM
TO THE HEREFORDSHIRE BEACON IN THE MALVERN HILLS

WORCESTERSHIRE AND HEREFORDSHIRE

SUMMER 1974

The purity of the natural landscape and the clarity of simple language are two things that Hamish Fulton wishes to convey in his work. But the most important thing to him is being in and walking through the landscape. The camera helps him record and represent that experience. The apparent naïvety of the activity confounds the sophisticates of the art establishment, but its raw simplicity comes over in his pieces – they are dignified and full of wonder

if you do not want to play the art gallery 'game', or are suspicious of the dealers' aims.

For example, you can put photographs in books which can be made easily available to the public at reasonable prices; you can explore the potential of the postcard and the poster. In most cases there will be very little loss of conventional photographic 'quality'. The *idea* should have quality, not the product. The preciousness of the 'fine' object and the limited edition strategy is anathema as it smacks of those bourgeois sentiments which put a monetary/rarity value on everything. Photographic prints can, in theory, be produced *ad infinitum*, which ruins the 'uniqueness' marketing ploy. Though it must be said that the *avante-garde* painters and sculptors, who now use photography, still only produce one or two prints from each negative.

The 'preciousness' of the artist/photographer as a special person reflecting, but somehow apart from, the real world, is seen to be a stereotype as archaic as the French beret and smock image. The artist/photographer is part of a 'system' which will always be political in nature, whether he or she likes it or not. The art that is in galleries – which probably only reaches a privileged few – is not the only art-form available. Most people are more directly affected by the visual impact of newspapers, magazines, television, advertisements, and posters than we are by what is hung on gallery and museum walls.

In photography it is very difficult – and this is one of its attractions – for the practitioner to avoid coming into close contact with the subject. This provides an ideal opportunity to experience at first-hand what is happening in the world and

The camera is a machine and many avant-garde *artists see its apparent mechanistic limitations as a challenge. To understand and demystify, by analysis, fits in with the increasing interest in information theory, logic, mathematics and new technologies. Here, former sculptor John Hilliard uses photography to discuss photography. He has examined in many of his pieces things like shutter speed, focus, aperture and exposure, in order to pedantically celebrate the process. In* Ten Runs Past a Fixed Point – 1/500 to 1 sec, *two actions take place simultaneously. While Hilliard is running with the camera, taking a photograph at a particular speed, a second person is taking photographs of him in action*

What does possession mean to you?

7% of our population own 84% of our wealth

The Economist, 15 January 1966

Advertisements and posters affect us more than what hangs in art galleries. Vic Burgin uses posters (and photographic prints that look like posters) to turn the language of advertising back on itself, to reveal what he sees as the artifices in capitalist society. He feels we are unaware of this often subliminal media manipulation. For Burgin 'the photograph is a sign, or more correctly, a complex of signs, used to communicate a message'. His 'message' is political because, he would argue, everybody is affected by political decisions, so we cannot afford the luxury of being apolitical

Nuclear power
The father gives his kind command,
the mother joins, approves;
the children all attentive stand,
then each obedient moves.

a) *Forlorn child (innocent victim), 1968*

b) *Mother and baby (Madonna and child), 1971*

d) *Depressed family group (object of pity), 1971*

c) *Anxious old age pensioner (helpless innocent), 1971*

e) *Resigned father (victim of society), 1971*

How I'd really like to be remembered!

This pastiche of a glamour-photography session highlights the way these sort of pictures are often read. The woman is portrayed stereotypically as being sexually available. Our blind acceptance of this cliché ignores the political implications of this kind of glamour photography. The woman is de-personalised and 'de-classed' (Jo Spence/Photography Workshop)

Reading the 'signs' in photographs is something Nick Hedges has done in his work for 'Shelter', the housing charity, for whom he was once a staff photographer. He found that many of the pictures his bosses used fitted into rather patronising stereotypes of the deprived working class. Images that, as Hedges puts it: 'conformed to a vague woolly middle-of-the-road liberalism'. The public accepted a certain kind of truth from an organisation like 'Shelter' because most people realise that a charity 'wears its propaganda on its sleeve' (Photography/Politics: One)

eventually to reflect it through your photographic work. Many people find art's continuous obsession with itself – art for art's sake – disturbing and socially inappropriate. They feel that art should concern itself more with political reality and less with introspection or being successful in the 'star' system so beloved by the dealers and the media.

Abdication of political responsibility may appear to be an innocent gesture, but it can often have unfortunate implications if it is not thought out. The photographer cannot evade the social and contextual ramifications of his or her work. It is no good blaming the political – or any other – system for our bruises, and then recoiling into the comparatively safe harbour of individualism. The photographer may be just as much a symptom of the political system as he, or she, is a victim. It is

121

Community photography projects are usually set up to develop the use of the medium as a tool for education and communication within the community. One of the first such projects was initiated at the Blackfriars Settlement, London. Its workers aim to teach local people photographic skills so they may have creative and educational experiences not normally available to them. The project also functions as a photographic resource for groups and individuals in the area (Caro Webb, Blackfriars Photography Project)

somewhat ironic (although the cynics would say it is sadly inevitable) to see the photographs from the *avante-garde* Conceptualists, and other camp followers, appearing on gallery walls and selling for not inconsiderable amounts of money. The paradox of artists and photographers selling work in galleries – or seeking employment in art colleges, so they can 'escape' from the conventions and the prostitution of the art world – may be amusing, or pathetic, depending on your point of view; but survival is survival.

Symbolism in photography

There is no point in espousing the cause of political awareness if photographers and photography users do not understand the significance of the images in the first place. Investigating the symbolism of photography – *semiology* – can help. A semiologist not only identifies the possible significance of the objects in photographs, but also tries to analyse why the photographer 'arranged' them that way. Some objects have particular symbolic significance individually, but when combined with other objects in a photograph may have a different overall significance. Our sense of 'reality' and existence is produced by a combination of symbols and images which form a language.

The *context* in which photographs are used is also critical. A great many photographs produced for a mass audience, via newspapers and magazines, are quite often put on gallery walls with little explanation or evidence of the original form in which they were seen. We are now so familiar with the insensitive juxtapositioning in magazines of starving Africans or Asians and sleek fashion models, that they seem to have become stereotypes inhabiting the same 'glossy' world.

The significance of the symbols in photographs is difficult to positively identify because photography can only give you a surface representation. To break through the surface in order to 'find' verifiable explanations, or answers to anything – without supplementary information – is impossible. This is why many *avant-garde* photographers rely heavily on the attachment of text to their pictures.

These written explanations are often attached to the photographs in an attempt to demystify the specific image and Art in general. The aim is to enable the viewer to understand the photographer's point of view. They often seem to state the obvious thus taking away any reliance on intuition, or previous historical knowledge of art. Anti-art photographers seek to strip photography of its aesthetic trappings, preferring instead to concentrate on its socio-political function.

But how can the work of the photo-journalist or the art photographer be socially relevant to the majority of the population? How can photographs which only represent the surface reality of things, change anything in society? Should photography be used for political ends anyway?

Many photographers have chosen to reject the 'normal' career roles of photography, and have refused to enter the frequently dispiriting and compromising competition for jobs. Instead, some have become involved with community groups and teaching projects.

Community photography

Community photography has many faces. It can, for example, help children and young adults express themselves when other means, such as writing, have failed. By studying the medium, young people can see not only how it is used in the world to influence them, but also how they may be able to influence others with their photographs. If there are serious social problems in a city, for instance, photographs can be used to illustrate how necessary it is for something to be done. This becomes more relevant if the photography is done by those who live there, rather than by a professional photographer from outside the community.

Not only can problems such as poverty, unemployment, homelessness and alcoholism be documented, but local photographers can help with campaigns initiated to effect changes such as amenity planning. Photography by its believability, can help make people more aware of problems by visually identifying them. The public's faith in the verisimilitude of photography can be used to great advantage – the dangers of naked *or* subtle propaganda notwithstanding. Photographs taken in the community should also be displayed there: in shopping areas, public thoroughfares, local libraries, leisure centres and so on. Discussions can be held on local matters with photographs as evidence.

Community newspapers can also be successful in communicating important local stories and information. Their concern is their readers. They also aim to reflect the effects of social problems, in

order to illuminate the political cause. They believe that for every social problem there is a political cure. Of course, a great many community activities involving photography do not have party political tags attached to them, but they can never be removed from politics.

Photography as propaganda

The use of photography as propaganda is more obviously seen in those groups with much 'sharper' political ideologies than the ones you find in community ventures. Feminism, for instance, does not have to look far for examples of photography used in the service of sexism. Any newsagents will provide you with all the evidence you need. If you are genuinely interested in female nude photography, how do you get over the hurdle of perpetuating the stereotype of woman as an erotic object? This question would never have been considered before the feminists drew attention to it with photographic evidence from magazines and advertisements to back up their arguments.

Ideological manipulation – often for the highest of motives – is a fact of life that we are obviously aware of when the 'message' is overt; but it is often on a subliminal level. The bent figure, with head down, wearing dirty clothes, in an industrial setting, could symbolise 'the oppression of the working class', if used in the correct political context. If the person is leaning on a spade, it could symbolise, in another context, 'the lazy worker who has helped bring about our economic decline'. Even subtler is the use of camera angle. If you photograph a person staring straight ahead, from slightly below, pointing the camera upwards, you can imbue that individual – whether peasant or plutocrat – with a convincing nobility or

Active feminists use photography as an anti-sexist weapon, and as a way to examine the role and representation of women in our society. To Angela Kelly, feminism is a political movement, as the first self-portrait overtly indicates. But the picture also shows an apparently genderless person. The sexual illusion is continued in the second image, which shows a 'transparent' nude figure posing in a conventionally 'attractive' way (note the gilt shoes) – available, but insubstantial. The photographer obviously appreciates the medium for its unique inherent qualities, as well as for its propagandistic usefulness

Photography can easily be manipulated by the media and we should be aware that we may not be shown the 'truth' in the photographs we see. This picture could be describing the archaic working conditions of an iron foundry, on one hand, or a worker toasting bread, instead of working, on the other. The subject can appear to be either the 'abused' or the 'abuser'. It all depends on how you interpret the images, or more particularly, how you are led to interpret them by their context, or via the words that accompany them (Paul Hill)

menacing demeanour. A similar angle used on young, handsome men, with blonde hair blowing in the breeze, was used by the Nazis to extol the wholesome virtues of racial purity. This effect works because subconsciously we are used to looking up to our 'betters', who sit above us on platforms in halls and classrooms, or whose likenesses reside in larger-than-life statues.

The idealised, somewhat reverential, view of the 'noble/peasant/leader/savage/visionary etc.', may seem archaically romantic to us nowadays, probably because of the façade-piercing work done by television. That flickering picture in the corner of the front-room may hypnotise, but it can also deflate, when it has a mind to.

Sensational exposé-conscious *media* is probably preferable to the controlled sort that exists in many countries only to expound the virtues of the government and the sort of Utopia 'we have in our country'. Cosy photo-essays appear in magazines (government sponsored) about hard-working families who respect the system they live under and who are quite prepared to toil for the good of the nation. Stylistically, the approach may seem to resemble objective journalism, but it is still political propaganda which affirms rather than challenges. But the 'free' press can also give journalists and proprietors the freedom to con and corrupt; which makes the understanding of the symbolism in photo-essays and picture stories all the more vital. *Visual 'literacy'* may be more universally important than polemics in the long run. If you understand the significance of photographs, then you may be able to utilise this knowledge in order to communicate more effectively and more honestly.

The subtle use of camera-angle subconsciously affects our reading of photographs of people. The low angle can increase the 'nobility' and larger-than-life character of many Very Important Persons, as the first picture, of an aristocratic, publishing magnate, demonstrates. Our 'betters', nowadays, are the media pundits and TV personalities, like Malcolm Muggeridge (opposite). But images, whether they are on a piece of paper or a flickering screen, eventually fade. Ideas, however, live on because they reside in the mind – and no-one can photograph that! (Paul Hill)

Conclusion

How photographers deal with their medium and its outlets, varies from nation to nation. Photographers are often anonymous in communist countries because the 'system' believes they should be happy to work selflessly for the State, while photographers in capitalist countries are noticeably seduced by the 'star' system and 'fame-and-fortune' incentives.

You should never consider that the political, or intellectual, *intent* of your pictures is above question. Never dismiss out of hand those ideological directions that instinctively make your hackles rise. Find out what puts you off, and also think about what may put people off your work. Are your photographs, for instance, appropriate to the audience that is destined to see them? Are they in a form (i.e. gallery prints, books etc.) which communicates their meaning successfully?

Do you consider the craft aspects carefully when executing your work? Will the 'fine' print get in the way of communicating your ideas? Finally, consider whether the photographic forms and approaches you use are so familiar to viewers and readers that they have become 'invisible' and, therefore, incapable of effecting, or affecting, social change, entrenched ideologies, or even the emotions.

Photography can be a very difficult and humbling medium, but the study and practice of it must always be *enjoyed* if it is to be at all illuminating.

126

INDEX

'Accidents', 21
Action pictures, 77
Advertisements, 119
Aestheticism, 115
Album, 59
Ambiguity, 28, 91, 104
Angles, 6, 124, 126
Anthropologists, 60
'Anti-art', 115
Archive, 47
Art, 33, 111, 121, 123
  centre, 46
  gallery, 43, 118
  history, 35
  influence on photography, 35
  institutions, 115
  market, 115
  photography, 104
  world, 114, 115
Audience, 43, 126
Avant-garde, 54, 115, 118, 123

Beauty, 83, 84, 89
Blackfriars Settlement, 122
Blurred (photographs), 38, 40
Books, 50
Bromide (printing papers), 89
Buildings, 86
'Burning-in' (printing), 28

Camera(s), 1, 3
  formats (types), 2
  obscura, 33
  vision, 1
Campaigns, 123
Canaletto, 34
Capitalist, 126
Caption(s), 8, 43, 77
Chiaroscuro, 87
Chloro-bromide (printing papers), 89
Close-up, 15
Conceptual, 35
Conceptualists, 114, 115, 123
Commission, 47, 50
Communication, 71
Communist, 126
Community, 122, 123
Composition, 2, 18
Conservation, 82, 84
  (prints), 47
Contact print, 24, 28
'Contacts', 24

Content, 43, 65
Context, 43, 123, 124
Contrast (photographic papers), 29
Courbet, 35
Cropping, 28

Dada(ism), 35, 114, 115
Dealers (art), 115, 118
Debuffet, 33
'Decisive moment', xii
'Decorative objects', 111
Development, over-, 26
Diaries (visual), 28
Disaster, 77
Document, 68
Documentary, 68, 104, 115
'Dodging' (printing), 28

Editions, limited, 115, 118
Enlargement, 5
Enlarging (printing), 26, 28
Environment, 89
'Equivalent(s)', 98, 99
Evidence, 43, 59
Exhibition, 46, 47
Experimental, 21
Exposure, 5, 26
  meter, 9, 21
  over-, 26
Eyes, 60

Family, the, 93
Feminism, 124
Film (formats), 2
'Fine' (print), 86, 97
Focal point, 14
Form, 43, 65
Frame, the, 5, 108
French Revolution, the, 35
Freud, 104

Galleries, 44, 103
Glamour, 121
Gombrich, Prof. Ernst, 33
'Grain', 5, 56
Guide-books, 81

'Highlights', 23, 26
Historians, 60
Humour, 110

Illusion, 12
Impressionists, The, 35
Individualism, 121
Industrialisation, 35, 82
Information, 76
'Introspective mode', 104

Journalism, 40, 52, 125
Juxtapositioning, 18, 20, 103

Landscape(s), 82, 83, 86, 89, 97, 104,
  112, 113, 116, 117
Lenses, 2, 6, 7, 40
Life (magazine), 36
Light, 9, 12, 21, 29, 108
'Literacy', 'visual', 125
Literature, 38
'Luminosity', 89

Magazines, 52
  news, 71
Media, 125
Metaphors, 15, 91, 93
Millet, 35
'Modernist formalism', 11
Monographs, 50
Motifs, 92, 100
Mounting, 47
Movement, 38
Movies, 38
Museum(s), 46, 47, 103, 118

Nadar, 35
Narrative, 38, 69, 76
National Front, 64, 78
National parks, 82
Nature, 81, 82, 96
Nazis, 125
Negative(s), 23, 24, 25, 26, 28
News, 52
Newspapers, 52, 53, 54, 123
Newsprint, 56

'Otherness', 96

Painting, 33, 34, 35
Panning, 40, 41
Papers, photographic, 29, 89

Performances, 115
Personal expression, 38
Photo-essay(s), 38, 71, 72, 76, 125
Photo-journalism, 52
Photo-murals, 56
Photo-realism, 35
Plane, picture, 11, 14
Polemics, 125
Police, 60
Political, 115, 121, 123, 124, 126
Picturesque, 84
Picture stories, 71, 125
Portfolio(s), 47, 98
Portrait(s), 60, 61, 64, 65
Postcard, 118
Posters, 56, 118, 119
Post-visualisation, 21, 28, 98
Pre-Raphaelite(s), 32, 33
'Presence', 98
Pre-visualisation, 1
Print, the, 29, 89, 97, 115
Propaganda, 77, 121, 123, 124
Psychological, 92, 98, 99
Psychologists, 60
Publicity, 60
Publishing, 47, 50

Reading (photographs), 1
Representation, 59
Reproduction, 47, 56
Romantic, 81

Science, 96, 115
'Scoop', 53
'Self', 92
Self-expression, 92
Self-portrait, 92
Semiotics, 115
Semiology, 123
Sequencing (prints), 31, 38, 98
Shadows, 12
Shelter, 121
Snapshot(s), 59, 60
Society, 96
Sociologists, 60
Souvenirs, 59, 60
'Spirit of place', 97
Statement, 31
Stereotypes, 121, 123, 124
Stieglitz, Alfred, 60
'Straight' (approach), 86
Students (art), 115
Subjective, 92
Surrealism, 35, 104, 106
Symbolism, 92, 97, 110, 123
Symbols, 15

Talbot, Henry Fox, 34
Television, 38, 125

Theme, a, 29
Three-dimensional, 11
Title(s), 8, 42, 43, 44
Tones, 9, 12, 14, 15
Topographical, 80, 112
'Topographics', 111
Topography, 86
Transcend(ant), 97, 99
Two-dimensional, 11, 12

Vantage point, 8
Victoria, Queen, 35
View camera(s), 2, 86
Viewfinder, 5
Viewing systems, 2

War, 77
Warhol, Andy, 114
Wordsworth, William, 38

Names of photographers and artists

Adams, Robert, 112
Arnatt, Keith, 114

Baker, Deborah, 62, 105
Baird, Kenneth, 31
Baltz, Lewis, 85, 88
Bedford, Francis, 81
Blakemore, John, 18, 21, 97
Brandt, Bill, 87, 107
Bubbles, Barney, 49
Burgin, Vic, 119

Calderon, P. H., 32
Callahan, Harry, 27, 113
Campbell, Bryn, 76
Cartier-Bresson, Henri, xii
Caponigro, Paul, 26, 99
Charity, John, 11, 13
Cooper, Mary, 67
Cooper, Thomas, 42, 96

Duchamp, Marcel, 34

Fulton, Hamish, 117

Gibson, Ralph, 17, 106
Godwin, Fay, 48, 83
Gowin, Emmet, 94, 95
Griffin, Brian, 49, 55, 111

Hedges, Nick, 69, 70, 71, 120
Hill, Paul, 4, 5, 6, 7, 8, 9, 10, 12, 14, 15,
    19, 22, 25, 28, 30, 39, 40, 41, 45, 46,
    52, 54, 59, 63, 64, 65, 68, 72–75,
    89, 90, 91, 93, 100, 101, 102, 103,
    105, 108, 112, 125, 126, 127
Hilliard, John, 118
Hughes, Ted, 48
Hurn, David, 20

Jones-Griffiths, Philip, 50

Kelly, Angela, 92, 124

Long, Richard, 116

Marey, Etienne Jules, 34
McCormick, Ron, 84
McCullin, Don, 77
Michals, Duane, 44
Moore, Raymond, 16, 109
Mulvany, John, 24
Myers, John, 66

Ormerod, Michael, 88

Palmer, Roger, 42
Parslow, Jamie, 62

Ray-Jones, Tony, 27
Robinson, Henry Peach, 33

Sadler, Richard, 8
Sorgi, I. Russell, 51
Smith, Graham, 85
Spence, Jo, 60, 121
Steele-Perkins, Chris, 78, 79
Strand, Paul, 86

Veigaard, Paul Erik, 20

Washburn, Bradford, 82
Webb, Caro, 122
Weston, Edward, 86
White, Minor, 98
Wilson, G. Washington, 80
Wolmuth, Philip, 43